# Last Ride

## A Gideon Johann Western
## Book 4

### By
### Duane Boehm

Last Ride: A Gideon Johann Western Book 4

For more information or permission contact: boehmduane@gmail.com

ISBN: 1-52287-834-3

## Other Books by Duane Boehm

*In Just One Moment*
*Last Stand: A Gideon Johann Western Book 1*
*Last Chance: A Gideon Johann Western Book 2*
*Last Hope: A Gideon Johann Western Book 3*
*Last Breath: A Gideon Johann Western Book 5*
*Wanted: A Collection of Western Stories (7 authors)*

*In memory of Grandpa Boehm for the love of music and the guitar*

# Chapter 1

Ethan Oakes walked into the jail in Last Stand, Colorado and found his longtime friend, Sheriff Gideon Johann, dusting the shelves in his office. Gideon looked up at him sheepishly, failing to conceal his embarrassment at getting caught in the act of cleaning.

The two men's friendship went back to childhood with an eighteen-year interruption when Gideon disappeared after the war. Found wounded outside of Last Stand, Gideon lay near dead and a bitter man. With the help of old friends and rekindled love, his transformation in the last couple of years had been nothing short of miraculous. He had made the most of his second chance in life at finding happiness.

"If I had known that you were getting all domesticated, I would have loaned you one of Sarah's aprons," Ethan said.

"You're a fine one to talk. Sarah says jump and you say how high. You'd best stick to ranching and preaching. Your jokes are a little stale," Gideon said.

Grinning, Ethan took off his hat and eased his large frame into the chair facing the desk. "Why don't you get Finnie to do that? What good is a deputy if you can't make him do the dirty work?" he asked.

"I'd rather do it myself than listen to him. Do you know how annoying an Irish brogue can be when it's whining?" Gideon said as he joined Ethan at the desk.

"You've got a point there. He is a feisty little man," Ethan said.

"What brings you to town?" Gideon asked.

"Blackie is supposed to have that wagon wheel repaired that Zack smashed into a rock. That boy was a pretty good ranch hand until he married your daughter. I think he daydreams about what's waiting for him at home these days. I will say though that marriage has put some giddy-up into his step," Ethan said.

Zack had married Gideon's daughter Joann in the spring. The sheriff had only learned that he and Abby had a child upon his return to Last Stand. After an awkward beginning, he and Joann had grown close until they now had a true father and daughter relationship.

"Ethan, the last thing in the world that I want to know about is Zack being anxious to get home to Joann. I'd just as soon not think about those things," Gideon said and rubbed the one-inch vertical scar on his cheekbone made courtesy of a rebel sabre.

Ethan let out a laugh. "You'll probably be a granddad before you know it."

"What's with you? You really are full of yourself today. I'm not ready to be a grandpa. I got my hands full with Chance. Since he began to walk, he about wears out Abby and me. I didn't know that a ten-month-old could get into so many things. Does it get any easier?" Gideon said.

"Quit your complaining. You love it and you know it," Ethan said.

"I didn't say that I didn't. I just never imagined that he would be so much work. He just goes and goes until he literally drops to the floor and falls asleep," Gideon said.

Wanting to change the subject, Ethan grew serious and straightened his posture. "Gideon, I wanted to let you know about something that I saw yesterday. That bull that I was so proud of when I showed him off to you, well, he has started getting rambling fever bad. Zack and I have been chasing him all over the countryside. Yesterday, we found him clear over by Moccasin Cave. I saw some riders taking their horses into it. They didn't see us. We were off in the brush, but they sure looked suspicious to me. I think that maybe there were five of them,"

Ethan's news caused Gideon to mull the information over a moment before speaking. "That's not really a place that you would make camp in unless you were caught in a rain storm. It surely doesn't sound right. I got a dispatch the other day that said the Cooper Gang out of Missouri had been chased into Colorado. They went on a crime spree all over Kansas. Rumor has it that Weasel Willie Trucks rides with them. I wonder if it's them and he led them here."

Ethan and Gideon had gone to school with Weasel Trucks. The nickname came from his close-set eyes and pointy nose. He had always been a scroungy, dirty, young man that seemed to attract trouble. Small in stature and wiry, he stood fearless in a fight no matter the size of the opponent, and had often been on the receiving end of a beating.

"We always said that Weasel would steal anything that wasn't fastened down and that Frank DeVille would swindle anybody out of their last dollar," Ethan said.

"And we were right. Frank's ways finally caught up with him and I expect that Weasel's will do the same. Finnie and I will ride out there and check out things. That Cooper Gang is supposed to be some bad men. I hope we are wrong about our suspicions," Gideon said.

"I need to get going, but I thought that you should know about it," Ethan said as he arose from the chair.

Deputy Finnegan Ford walked into the jail. Short in stature, with shoulders as broad as Ethan's, he stood a foot shorter than the rancher. A trained boxer, his sinewy body belied his good nature. In his heavy Irish accent, he said, "Top of the morning to you, Ethan."

"Good morning, Finnie. Good to see you. I hope that I keep seeing you and Mary at church," Ethan said.

Mary owned the Last Stand Last Chance Saloon. Twenty-eight years old, she was petite and pretty with black hair. Raised in an orphanage, her husband had been murdered after they moved to Last Stand. She had gone into the whoring business to make a living before inheriting the saloon. Finnie and she seemed to make an odd pair, especially considering that when Gideon dragged his old war buddy to town, Finnie was a down-and-out drunk. Given the choice between whiskey and Mary, Finnie had chosen Mary. Somehow they had managed to bury the misfortunes of their pasts to allow them to find happiness together. He had been sober a year and lived with her in the saloon though they had never gotten around to marriage.

"I think I've gotten Mary to quit worrying about what other people think of us coming. We're not there for them anyway. I come mainly to marvel at you. It's not often that somebody as big as you is not dumber than a box of rocks," Finnie said with a chuckle.

"You dwarfs always have a mean streak in you. I think it comes from having to stand on your tiptoes so much," Ethan said and grinned, proud of his comeback.

Gideon stood and grabbed his hat. "Okay, gentlemen, I can think of nothing that I'd rather do than listen to you two jaw at each other all day, but I have work to do."

# Chapter 2

Moccasin Cave sat northeast of Last Stand in some of the roughest, most barren land in the area. No homesteads or ranches were near the cave and the spot was seldom traveled. Old-timers claimed that the first time white settlers explored the cave, they found six pair of moccasins all lined up together. The mystery remained unresolved, but the name stuck. The walls remained decorated with crude figurines, and broken pieces of pottery littered the floor. Legend had it that an Indian ghost haunted the cavern. A spring trickled out of the cave wall and made a pool of fresh water before running deeper into the cave, making it an ideal place to hole up.

After lunch, Gideon and Finnie rode out of town towards the cave. The cloudless sky and relentless sun made for a warm August day. For most of the trip, the land they rode across was grassland dotted with hills and ridges and all of it still green from the summer rains. The mountains loomed all around in the background like guardians of all below them. They had a good distance to travel and alternated between putting the horses into a lope and a walk.

As they pulled the horses to a walk, Gideon asked, "Are you ever going to ask Mary to marry you?"

Finnie looked at Gideon in surprise. "You're getting just a wee-bit personal there, aren't you?" he asked.

Gideon rolled his eyes. "Oh, good God, is there anything we don't know about each other? Answer the damn question."

Finnie sat up in his saddle and gave Gideon a dirty look. "Mary and I are very happy. Why would the proprietor of a booming saloon want to marry a deputy? She probably earns more than me and you put together."

"In other words, you're afraid to ask her. You sound as bad as Zack did when he was afraid to court Joann because he didn't think that he was worthy of her. Mary doesn't give a damn about the money and you know it. She just wants to be happy and loved. Does her past make you skittish about marrying her?" Gideon said.

"I don't care one bit that she was a whore. I was a drunk. Neither of us have pasts that are worth writing home about. I'm just afraid that she would say no and I don't want to ruin what we have," Finnie said.

"You and Zack really are alike. I'm surprised either one of you has ever been kissed. Both of you have risked your lives to come to my aid when I was in trouble and yet you have to be preached to when it comes to dealing with women," Gideon said.

Knowing Gideon's discomfort at being teased about the newlywed bliss of Zack and Joann, Finnie went for the jugular to shut him up. "I wouldn't worry about Zack these days. The way he walks around with that goofy smile on his face, I think that he is getting all the loving that he can handle."

The two men rode the rest of the trip in agitated silence. Reaching the spot where the brush and trees stopped, Gideon pulled a spyglass from his saddlebag before dismounting. The land between them and the cave lay flat and all rock, providing a clear view of the opening. About an eighth of a mile separated them, and with the naked eye they could see wisps of smoke drifting from the cave.

"Looks like they're still here or that ghost that lives there is cooking a meal," Finnie said.

Gideon chortled. "I don't think that's a ghost, but I dare say it is somebody that is up to no good."

"True. I've never known a ghost to make a fire, but back in the old country where things were civilized centuries before a white man ever set foot over here, ghost were as thick as flies on cow dung," Finnie said.

Giggling, Gideon slapped his leg. "Only you could work ghost and cow shit into the same sentence. You have a way with words, I'll give you that. We'll just sit here and watch what goes on."

The sun sank halfway behind the horizon and still no one had emerged from the cave. Finnie sat with his lap covered in a pile of shavings from whittling a batch of toothpicks while Gideon watched the cave and paced. Catching sight of some movement at the mouth of the cavern, he stopped in his tracks and raised the spyglass to study the situation.

"Well, I'll be. It is Weasel. I'd recognize those close-set eyes and that upturned, pointy nose anywhere no matter how many years it'd been since I saw him. Looks like he's taking the horses out to pasture for the night. I count five of them," Gideon said.

"So what's our plan?" Finnie asked as he stood and brushed off the shavings.

"He's headed east. There's some decent grass about a half mile that direction once you get past the rock and then some pines. We'll ride over there and make sure that we know where he left the horses and then come back before light and be ready," Gideon said.

"You mean I have to be back here before light? I'll have to get up at three in the morning. These outlaws had better surrender peacefully for I'll be in an ill mood. I'll show them the wrath of the Irish. We should've made plans to camp the night," Finnie groused.

"If we didn't have women that'd be worrying about us, we'd rough it for the night. I've given Abby enough troubles to last a lifetime and I don't plan to add to it," Gideon said.

Back in their youth, Gideon and Abby had been sweethearts. She had wed another man in the years that Gideon had gone missing and found herself in an unhappy marriage. After Gideon returned, they realized they still had feelings for each other and eventually she divorced Marcus and married Gideon.

Finnie untied the horses and walked them over to Gideon.

"It is a burden to be as lovable as us two," Finnie said as he mounted his horse.

Gideon and Finnie made a circle headed towards the east and a little north. They rode at a leisurely pace to allow Weasel plenty of time to return to the cave. Reaching the pines, they tied the horses and pulled their rifles from their scabbards. Gideon led the way as they traipsed through a couple hundred feet of pines until they reached a clearing where they found the horses staked on a line.

"We'll meet at five tomorrow morning where we now have our horses tied and then we'll hide all the horses and wait for someone to come get them. It'll be just like the old days in the war when we got to use the element of surprise. You can head back to town and I'm headed home," Gideon said.

"The biggest surprise will be if I don't shoot you for getting me up so early," Finnie said before spinning around and walking back towards their horses.

∞

Gideon stood waiting as Finnie rode up in the predawn morning. He contemplated jumping out to scare the Irishman but thought better of it, having no desire to catch one of Finnie's famous right-hooks as his deputy defended himself against a perceived ghost.

"Over here, Finnie," Gideon whispered.

"I was afraid I wasn't going to find this place in the dark," Finnie said.

"We'll walk our horses through the trees and then go hide all of them and then we'll wait in the pines until somebody comes to retrieve them," Gideon said.

"Do you think we have time before they get here?" Finnie asked.

"Have you ever known of an outlaw that wasn't lazy? They don't like work. We'll be starving by the time they get here," Gideon said as he started maneuvering through the pines with very little light in which to see.

They hid the string of horses as well as their own mounts on the backside of a nearby ridge and began walking back to the pines. The cool morning lent itself to a brisk pace without working up a sweat. As they walked, the sky lightened enough that the world looked as if it were painted in gray.

Reaching the trees, Gideon said, "Right here is the path. You get behind that pine and I'll get behind the one on the other side. We'll wait for somebody to show up and take them. It should be easy."

"And then what?" Finnie asked.

"The rest of them will come looking for him either together or one by one. We'll wait for them on the front side. They'll be coming across all that rock and there won't be any place for them to hide," Gideon said as he took his place behind the pine.

The sun had topped the horizon by the time they heard the sound of someone coming, making more noise than a bull on a rampage. The man walked into the clearing and stopped.

"Oh, shit. Somebody stole the horses," he said aloud.

Gideon stealthily maneuvered around the pine and walked up behind the man, driving the butt of his Winchester between his quarry's shoulder blades and sending the outlaw nose first into the ground. Cocking his rifle, Gideon pushed the barrel against the man's skull behind his ear.

"Weasel, I'm sure that I owed you that for something that you did back in school," Gideon said as he reached down and retrieved the outlaw's revolver from its holster. "Now roll over."

The outlaw complied with the order, studying the sheriff as Gideon stood over him with the rifle pointed at his upturned nose.

"Gideon Johann. I thought you was dead," Weasel said.

"Apparently not," Gideon said as he pulled a kerchief from his pocket. "Shove this into your mouth."

'It don't look none too clean. Does it got snot on it?" Weasel asked.

"I don't recall, but your only other option is that I kill you and then you're going to be tasting dirt," Gideon said as Finnie handed him his kerchief and some leather bindings he had retrieved from his saddlebag.

Weasel stuffed the cloth into his mouth before Gideon took the other kerchief and gagged him. The sheriff then tied Weasel's hands behind his back with the leather strips and hogtied them to his feet, leaving the outlaw helpless on his stomach in the grass.

"Let's take a walk to the other side," Gideon said to Finnie.

"What do you think happens now?" Finnie asked.

"Don't know. I haven't decided if I think that they'll come one at a time or all together. I wish they'd come one by one. Maybe we could waylay them all and not have to shoot anybody. That would be a good day. If they come scattered out, then you take the far right one and I'll take the left. We'll worry about the ones in the middle after that," Gideon said.

"I didn't bring enough leather to tie up all of them," Finnie remarked.

"That's probably the least of our worries," Gideon said as they reached the other side of the pines. The two men took cover fifteen yards on either side of the path entrance and waited.

Over an hour passed before they saw the four men in the distance walking towards them. They were scattered out and all carrying rifles as they searched for signs of Weasel. The men appeared nervous and edgy as they cautiously walked.

Gideon waited until the outlaws were no more than thirty yards away before shouting, "Throw down your guns and nobody gets hurt."

Three of men turned their heads to look at the man second from the left for apparent direction on what next to do. That outlaw raised his rifle, firing in the direction of Gideon's voice. Gideon's and Finnie's rifles roared like two sixteenth notes on a marching drum before the others had time to aim. The men on the far left and right flung backwards off their feet. The two remaining outlaws took off running to their left as Gideon and Finnie unloaded on them. Just before the two men reached a crop of rock, one of them dropped to the ground, but managed to jump up and limp to safety. They began firing wildly into the pines, forcing Gideon and Finnie to keep hugging the ground as the bullets tore through the branches. The two lawmen held their fire, waiting for a pause in the barrage.

"You two might as well surrender. There's no way that you can escape. Throw out your guns and stand with your hands in the air," Gideon shouted.

A shot zipped through the air, hitting the ground close enough to kick up dirt onto Gideon and pissing him off.

"Go to Hell," one of the outlaws yelled.

Gideon scampered back through the trees until he found Finnie crouched on the ground with his rifle trained towards the rocks.

Finnie looked over his shoulder. "What now? This could take all day and I'm hungry. They barely show themselves when they pop up and shoot. We might never get a decent shot. They'd only hit something if they got lucky."

"Why are you complaining? They don't even know where you are. All the shots are towards me, and last time I checked, a lucky shot kills the same as a well-aimed bullet," Gideon said.

for him. The outlaw pulled his pants down and turned so the doctor could see the wound. 'Is it bad?" he asked.

The doctor bent over and examined the injury. "I've seen cat scratches on children a lot worse than this and with a lot less bellyaching to boot. You might have fallen down in surprise, but that shot didn't knock you down. You can quit your limping now too," he said as he retrieved a bottle of iodine and dabbed the wound.

"Well, it felt bad," Bucktooth said defensively.

Doc looked towards Gideon and Finnie. "You two might want to invest in some spectacles or shotguns if you can't shoot any better than that."

Gideon grinned and rubbed the scar on his cheek. "I'm going to have to buy you a beer to get you in a better mood. Those two ran like jackrabbits. We got them all the same. This here is Bucktooth Cooper. You can tell everybody that you doctored a famous outlaw."

"He's not the first. Every one of them has been a whiner. Get him out of here," Doc snapped.

Finnie tipped his cap at the doctor. "Good day to you, you grouchy old sawbones," he said before they left with their prisoner.

After locking Bucktooth in a third cell, Gideon sat down at his desk, pulled a stack of wanted posters from his drawer, and began leafing through them. He pulled five of the posters out and set them to the side.

"Finnie, we've got twelve thousand dollars in reward money coming our way. I think we should split it four ways with Ethan and Zack. We wouldn't have known about the gang without them. Even with splitting it, it's more money than any of us has ever seen in our lifetime," Gideon said.

"You mean they pay the reward to the law too?   I thought that was just for bounty hunters," Finnie said.

"Yes, they do.  I'll telegraph the U.S. Marshal and see what he wants to do with these three," Gideon said.

Finnie began dancing the steps to an Irish jig and humming an accompanying melody.  "I'm as giddy as an Irishman locked in the wine cellar.  Finnegan Ford has three thousand dollars to his name and I'm Mary's equal now," he said before rushing Gideon and kissing him on the cheek before the sheriff had time to react.

"You ever do that again and that money is going to be used to bury your ass in a gold coffin.  Come on.  I'm going to telegraph the marshal and then I'll buy you that breakfast that I promised," Gideon said before pulling a clean kerchief from his pocket and vigorously rubbing his cheek.

By the time that the two men finished breakfast, Gideon was ready to get away from Finnie for a while. The Irishman, giddy with excitement over his change in fortune, had talked non-stop through the meal.  His thick Irish accent, spoken with rapid-fire speed in his elation, had sounded like a foreign language and Gideon understood little of what had been said.

After paying for the meal, Gideon said, "I'm going to ride out to see Ethan.  You stay here and keep an eye on the prisoners.  Stay away from those three.  I want us together when we deal with them."

"Don't you worry.  I'm not about to let my reward go anywhere.  My aim will be considerably more accurate this time if they try to pull something," Finnie said as sauntered off towards the jail.

Gideon rode to the cabin and found Ethan and Zack splitting firewood out in the yard while Sarah sat on the porch sewing.

Climbing down from his horse, Gideon said, "Looks like Sarah is cracking the whip around here. She's a mean one."

Sarah had played a big role in nursing Gideon back to health when he was found shot. They had never met up to that point in time, but still developed a sibling like relationship. He still sought out her counsel when he needed unvarnished advice. Sometimes her opinion might not be what he wanted to hear, but it was always the truth and he loved her dearly.

"And my hearing is just fine. Be good or you'll be joining them," Sarah said as she walked off the porch to greet Gideon. "What brings you out here?"

Waiting until the three of them had gathered in semicircle around him, Gideon said, "I got some good news. Finnie and I caught the Cooper Gang. We're going to split the reward with Ethan and Zack. That's three thousand dollars apiece. You can buy firewood with that kind of money."

Zack and Sarah stood looking dumbstruck while Ethan shifted his weight from one leg to the other, appearing uncomfortable.

"Gideon, you don't have to do that. You and Finnie are the ones that risked your life, not Zack and me," Ethan said.

"Nonsense. They could have been at Moccasin Cave for a year and nobody would have been any the wiser if you hadn't seen them or somebody could have happened along and gotten themselves killed. I don't need any more money than that anyways," Gideon said.

Sarah threw her arms around Gideon and hugged him. "I knew I nursed you back to health for a reason," she teased. "You and Abby are such dear friends."

"I'd make Ethan build on to the cabin with some of that money," Gideon said, grinning at Ethan.

"Well, who do you think that she is going get to help me if we do? You'll live to regret that suggestion," Ethan said.

Zack cleared his throat. "You'd really do that for me?" he asked.

"Well, since you're married to my daughter, it's kind of keeping it in the family. Knowing Joann, she'll probably want to spend all of it or not a nickel. I'm not sure which, but I'm sure she'll have an opinion one way or the other," Gideon said.

"I planned on telling you the next time I saw you that we got approved for our homestead. We should be able to really do things right with the reward. That money is going for the homestead and I don't care what Joann thinks about it," Zack said.

Gideon grinned at his son-in-law, remembering all the grief that his daughter had put upon Zack during their courtship. "My, my, my, have we grown a backbone, Zack?"

"You know how Joann is. She still gets her way plenty, but when I put my foot down, she listens. You can't be washy with that girl," Zack said.

Sarah smiled and shook her head while listening to Zack talk as if he were the one that figured out all by himself how to handle Joann, when in fact, she, Ethan, and Gideon had all told him time and again that the only way he was ever going to win Joann's hand was to hold his own with her.

"I need to get back to town. I'm waiting to hear back from the U.S. Marshal on what he wants to do with the prisoners," Gideon said as climbed upon his horse.

Ethan stepped forward, patting Gideon's horse on the neck. "Thank you, Gideon. This is a very generous thing that you are doing. I'm much obliged."

"Where would either one of us be without the other? It's my pleasure," Gideon said before wheeling the horse around and riding away.

Sarah looked at Zack and said, "You go on home to Joann and tell her the big news. This is worth celebrating. The wood can wait."

Zack glanced over at Ethan who stood glaring and obviously perturbed at his wife.

"Go ahead, Zack. I'm sure that Joann will be excited," Ethan said unenthusiastically.

"See you tomorrow," Zack said as he walked to his horse and rode away.

"Why did you do that? There's wood to chop. You won't think that's such a good idea when the cabin is cold this winter," Ethan complained.

Sarah sashayed towards the cabin looking over her shoulder and smiling. "I've never gone to bed with a rich man. Your son will be home in half an hour. You can stay out here and split wood or you can split ...," she said, letting her voice trail off into a giggle before disappearing into their home.

# Chapter 4

Raising a ten-month-old child was proving to be much more of a challenge than Abby Johann remembered it to be. The task seemed much easier with her daughter, Winnie, nearly a decade earlier. She found that she had much more patience with Chance than she had ever had with her daughter, but not the energy. Chance could give her a smile and get by with things that she would have never let fly with Winnie, but by the end of the day, she felt exhausted. He was a very active child, and since beginning to walk, into everything. Blaming the difference on the fact that the child was a boy, she refused to concede that her age had anything to do with the situation.

Joann, Abby's newlywed daughter, had started coming over on Wednesday mornings to watch her brother so that Abby could have a break and go visit with Ethan's wife Sarah. The two women had been friends for years and took comfort in each other's confidences in the challenges of life on a ranch. Lately, the two women had added Mary to their get-togethers. Finnie had taught her how to ride a horse and she had purchased her own, loving the freedom of riding and leaving her life in a saloon for a while.

The three women sat at Sarah's table drinking coffee. Abby had been talking for ten minutes about all the precocious things Chance was learning to do. She tended only to recall the joys of parenthood and not the challenges that fell by the wayside and become insignificant when she sat in the company of her friends. Looking up at Mary, she stopped mid-sentence at seeing tears in her friend's eyes.

"Mary, what's the matter?" Abby asked.

"I'm pretty sure I'm with child. I'm two weeks late and I'm usually like clockwork. I don't know what I'm going to do," Mary said and began sobbing.

Abby and Sarah exchanged glances, neither sure what next to say. Mary's life had been a series of tragedies before inheriting the saloon and meeting Finnie. She had survived her ordeals seemingly unscathed and her reaction caught them both off-guard.

Sarah leaned over the table and placed her hand on Mary's wrist. "Don't you want a baby, Mary?" she finally asked.

Mary used her sleeve to wipe her eyes. "Considering that I used to be a whore, I know that this may sound hard to believe, but I quit thinking about babies a long time ago. After being married to Eugene, and then with all the men I've been with since, I never once got pregnant. I figured I couldn't have children and put it out of my mind. I don't know what Finnie will do. He won't even ask me to marry him. What's he going to think about a baby? I'm afraid I will lose him."

"Has he ever mentioned children?" Abby asked.

"No, Finnie never says anything about our future and I don't either. It's like we're afraid to bring anything up as if it might all fall apart," Mary said.

Abby reached over and patted Mary's hand. "Finnie gave up the bottle for you and he was a pretty bad drunk. You know that you have to mean a lot to him. And he's great with kids. Look how he is around Winnie and Benjamin and the baby. I think he's just afraid that you'll say no if he asked you to marry him and I bet he'll be overjoyed with a baby. A baby can't be half as scary as giving up whiskey."

"I don't know," Mary said and started crying again.

"You have to tell him. I think everything is going to be fine," Sarah said.

"Even if he does want the baby, I'm not fit to be a mother. I was raised in an orphanage and I was a whore. What kind of mother would that make?" Mary said.

Sarah pointed her finger at Mary, shaking it with emphasis. "You'll be as good of a mother as you want to be. Your past has nothing to do with it. You have a responsibility to that child and you will be fine. Mary, you are a good person and we'll all be here for you just as you were for us. Abby and I know a thing or two about raising a child."

"I know I'll try, but there's so much to think about. A saloon is no place to raise a baby. What kind of life would that be? And you know that when the child gets older that somebody will tease it about its mother being a whore. I don't want my child to have a terrible childhood like I had," Mary said.

"You don't have to live in the saloon to run it. You and Finnie could get a house. You just need to tell him and figure out things. All the money that he has coming his way now should help a lot. I'm telling you right now though, lots of love fixes a whole lot of problems. I think that you will make a great mother," Abby said.

"What money?" Mary asked.

Sarah and Abby looked at each other, both regretting that the subject of the reward had been brought into the conversation.

"Finnie has reward money coming for helping capture the Cooper Gang. I figured that he told you. I shouldn't have said anything," Abby said.

"It's not like we are married. I don't share with him how much I make off the saloon. I guess he has a right to keep it to himself," Mary said, though her words didn't sound convincing.

"I'm sorry, Mary," Abby said.

"Do you think he is planning to take the money and run?" Mary asked.

"No. No. No. I don't think that there's any chance of that. Finnie's a good and honorable man. Just because he's short, don't go selling him short," Sarah said, trying to lighten the mood.

"Well, if I am pregnant, it's not like I'm not going to have it. I wouldn't ever do that, but I just don't know how this is all going to work out," Mary said.

"As a preacher's wife, I'm going to tell you to have a little faith in yourself, Finnie, and God. I'm betting on all of you," Sarah said.

# Chapter 5

U.S. Marshal Wilcox arrived in Last Stand accompanied by a deputy and a prison wagon. Gideon and Finnie had just finished feeding the prisoners their breakfast when the two men entered the jail. The marshal made for a dashing figure in black coat and string tie. He was tall and lanky with a bushy handlebar mustache and dark piercing eyes.

"Sheriff Johann, I'm Marshal Wilcox," Wilcox said as he extended his hand to Gideon.

Gideon shook his hand. "Glad to meet you, Marshal. This here is Deputy Finnegan Ford. I'll be glad to have you take those prisoners off my hands. They're a bellyaching bunch."

"You would have saved the government a considerable expense if you would have killed the whole gang," Wilcox said.

"I probably should have. James Cooper keeps threatening me with revenge for killing his brother," Gideon said.

"I don't expect Mr. Cooper will be spending another day on this earth as a free man. Can I have a look at the prisoners?" Wilcox said.

The marshal followed Gideon into the cell room. Wilcox took a quick glance at the men and walked out of the room without addressing the prisoners.

"That's the Cooper Gang alright. You're going to be taking my job one of these days if you keep bringing all these outlaws to justice. You've made quite a name for

LAST RIDE ● 28

yourself in the short time that you've been sheriff. I congratulate you," Wilcox said.

"Thank you, Marshal. I have the other two bodies in a cellar for you to identify them," Gideon said.

The four men walked to the cabinetmaker's shop and were led out back to the cellar. The cool room kept the bodies from decomposing rapidly, but the corpses still gave off a pungent stench when the lids to the coffins were lifted.

"That looks like Horace Cooper and Robert Hopkins to me. Let's get out of here. I'll lose my appetite for the rest of the day if I stay in here much longer. You can go ahead and bury them," the marshal instructed the cabinetmaker.

Once back at the jail, Marshal Wilcox said, "I'll get the paperwork for the reward finished when I get back. It will be sent in your name and you can do with it what you see fit. Let's get the prisoners and be on our way. I sure wish you would've just killed them,"

"Thank you, Marshal. Send the money in care of the Last Stand Bank. Next time I'll aim better for you," Gideon said.

The marshal smiled. "You do that," he said.

As the prisoners were led out of the jail, James Cooper turned to Gideon and said, "You think you've seen the last of me, but you're wrong. I'll kill you yet."

"You talk awfully big for a man in shackles," Gideon said and shoved James towards the wagon, almost making the prisoner fall.

As the two lawmen watched the marshal and his wagon of prisoners leave Last Stand, Gideon said, "I won't miss them, but I sure look forward to that reward. What are you going to do with your money, Finnie?"

"I haven't got it all figured out yet, but I'm working on it," Finnie said.

"If you were smart you'd buy a ring for Mary," Gideon said.

"You let me worry about that. You could always become my mother if you get tired of being sheriff," Finnie said.

"I'm just trying to help a friend," Gideon said.

"Has Mary said something to you?" Finnie asked brusquely.

"No. And I don't claim to be an expert on how the female mind works, but I know enough to figure out that Mary wants you to marry her," Gideon said.

"Considering that you left Abby to go fight a war and didn't get around to coming back and marrying her for eighteen years, I don't think that you have much room to talk," Finnie said and walked off down the street.

Finnie avoided the jail for the rest of the morning and waited until the lunch crowd left the Last Chance to go eat with Mary. He found her in an ill mood and gobbled his lunch down to get away as quickly as possible before making a beeline out of the saloon. She was upset with him over something and he didn't have a clue what he had done. When he asked her what was wrong, she had said nothing and then gave him one of those looks that inferred that he should know good and well what was bothering her. She was giving him a lot more credit than he deserved if she thought that he had any idea what he had done to upset her. He was beginning to wonder if she was tiring of his company with the way she behaved lately.

The stagecoach was due to arrive and Finnie walked to its arrival spot, taking a seat on the bench and waiting. Since becoming a full-time deputy, he liked to keep track of visitors to town. Usually the passengers were locals returning from a trip, but occasionally a stranger would arrive to pique his interest. He waited an hour before the stage finally pulled up. The rain from the night before made travel difficult and delayed the arrival.

The first passenger off the coach caught Finnie's attention. The man looked to be in his forties, medium height and build, with dark hair. Dressed in a finely tailored suit and derby hat, he looked to be from a big city and definitely stood out in the crowd. With his trunk retrieved, he walked past the coach towards the hotel, carrying himself in a regal manner. Arriving at his destination, he promptly disappeared inside the building.

Finnie flagged down one of the local passengers. "Did you catch the name of the man in the suit and where he is from?" he asked.

"His name is John and he's from Boston is all that I know. He asked a lot of questions about Last Stand, but he didn't talk about himself much at all," the passenger said.

Walking back to the jail, Finnie plopped down in a chair in front of the desk. "Some man from Boston arrived on the stagecoach. He's dressed in a fancy suit and walks as if he thinks he's a king or something. He looks as out of place as a virgin in a mining town saloon. Something is not right about it. I think we need to keep an eye on him," he said to Gideon.

"I'd be a lot more worried if he looked like an outlaw and was armed to the teeth. It's not against the law to visit the town. Maybe he's read about the west and wants to see it for himself. It may be unusual, but I've heard tales of little drunken Irishmen taking up residence with pretty little saloon owners. That's pretty hard to believe too," Gideon said, grinning at his friend.

"Well, you're funny today. Do you know why Mary's sore with me? She wasn't very pleasant at lunch," Finnie said.

"I haven't talked to her. Maybe she's getting tired of you or thinks that it's time that you marry her," Gideon said.

"Well, if memory serves me well, you had your chance to marry her and didn't," Finnie said.

"If Abby and I hadn't still had feelings for each other, I very well might have. You can thank me that she was still available," Gideon said to needle Finnie further.

"I'm going to quit talking to anybody today. Mary is mad and you're smug. If that man from Boston comes in here and shoots you, it will serve you right," Finnie said and stood to leave.

"Maybe Mary found out about the reward money. Did you tell her about it? News travels fast in this town, especially if Doc knows about it. She might be mad that you didn't share the news with her," Gideon said.

"She doesn't tell me about her finances. Why should I? It's not as if I actually have the money in my hand yet. And how would she find out?" Finnie said.

"Well, Abby and Sarah know about it and Mary spends Wednesdays with them. What do you think the odds are that the reward didn't come up in conversation?" Gideon said.

"Damn. When women get together, they make more noise than a chicken coop full of hens. I'm surprised that they don't nest on eggs," Finnie said.

"They kind of do. Ethan and I have the kids to prove it. That stuff can happen when you play with the hens," Gideon said as he rubbed his scar and chuckled.

"You are so funny. Maybe you'll be a grandpa rooster real soon then. I'll go keep the peace in this town while you sit here and think up some more jokes," Finnie said before dashing out the door.

Gideon finished logging his expenses before walking to the Last Chance. He sat down at his usual table and waited for Mary to bring a beer and join him.

Mary placed the beer on the table and sat down with him. "You haven't visited me this week. I thought that maybe you didn't love me anymore," she teased.

"I'm here now. How have you been?" Gideon said.

"I'm good. Business is booming," Mary said.

"I hear that you're peeved at Finnie. Trouble in paradise?" he said.

"At least I got his attention enough to make him talk to you about it. I heard about the reward money and I'm just disappointed that he didn't share the news with me. I don't tell him about my money, but I'd think he'd want to share big news like that. I also thought that he would've married me by now and you see what that got me," she said.

"I'm sure he will tell you in due time. Mary, he is afraid to ask you because he's afraid that you'll say no. Finnie might be a dried out deputy, but he still thinks of himself as the little drunk that I found in Animas City and he doesn't feel that he is your equal. I give him a hard time about it all the time and it doesn't do any good," Gideon said.

"That little idiot Irishman. I should just shoot him," Mary said before a ranch hand walked by reeking of body odor and cow shit. She covered her mouth with her hands and started retching.

"What's up with you? I'd think that you'd be used to that smell by now," he said before rubbing his chin and smiling. "Oh, my God, you're with child. Abby was the same way when she was carrying Chance. I finally got one on you instead of the other way around."

After the gagging stopped, Mary said, "Gideon Johann, keep your voice down. This isn't funny. I'm afraid Finnie will hightail it when he finds out. Having a baby is about the last thing that I ever expected to happen to me. It should be one of the happiest times in my life, but like usual, my life is never that simple."

"Mary, you need to talk to him. Finnegan Ford will do right by you, but you need to let him know. You've waited long enough for him to ask you. Just tell him. He won't run. In fact, I think that you'll make him a very happy man if you just lay your cards on the table. You'd save him from working up the nerve. He told me in the past that there was a time when he figured that he'd be married and have children. He just gave up on that dream, but it's about to become a reality," Gideon said.

"You really think so?' Mary asked.

"Yes, I do, and congratulations. I think that you'll make a wonderful momma," he said.

Mary stood and leaned over, kissing Gideon on the cheek. "You're a dear friend, but you'd better keep your mouth shut or I won't rescue you the next time somebody tries to kill you in my saloon."

# Chapter 6

The sky was cloudless, allowing the sun to dry out Last Stand after the downpour two nights earlier. Gideon precariously crossed the street, managing to navigate without slipping and making a spectacle of himself. The mud had sucked a shoe off his horse, Buck and he was headed to the livery stable to get a new one. Blackie, sweat drenched, was pounding a horseshoe on his anvil as Gideon approached.

"Blackie, I need to get you to reshod Buck. When can you get to it?" Gideon said.

"As soon as I get that gelding standing there finished, you'll be next," Blackie said.

"I'll go fetch him right now," Gideon said as he noticed a rider coming down the sloppy street in a gallop.

The rider, Carl Hill, spied Gideon and pulled his horse up hard in front of the stable, causing the animal's rear legs to slide under its self and crash down into a sitting position.

"Sheriff, I just came from Roy Weaver's place. I was supposed to help him repair his corral today. He and his squaw are hanging from a tree in their yard. It's a god-awful sight. They look to have been hanging there awhile," Carl said.

Roy Weaver, in his fifties, had lived and ranched around Last Stand all his life. He and the Ute woman that he called Sissy had been together nearly thirty years. The couple tended to keep to themselves, but was well liked in the community.

"When's the last time that you saw Roy?" Gideon asked.

"I was out there last week. I've been busy and we agreed that I'd come help him today," Carl said.

"I'll go and see about it. Carl, I'd appreciate it if you would keep this under your hat until I know more. There's no need to stir folks up until there's a reason," Gideon said.

"You have my word, Sheriff," Carl said before aiming his horse towards the Last Chance, apparently needing a drink to calm his nerves.

"Does Roy have any kin around here?" Gideon asked Blackie.

"His brother died a long time ago and I don't know where his two kids are. They're not around these here parts," Blackie said.

"Would you get me a buckboard ready and put some tarps in it? I'll go find Finnie and see if Doc wants to ride along," Gideon said.

"I'll do it. Go ahead and bring Buck back," Blackie said.

Gideon tracked down Finnie and then persuaded Doc to ride along after insisting that the bodies be examined and warning that he doubted that the remains would be fit for bringing into the doctor's office. Doc sat with Gideon on the bench seat as the sheriff maneuvered the team of horses on the three miles of muddy roads to the Weaver homestead. Finnie rode his own horse, having no desire to ride in the back of the wagon with the bodies on the return into town.

The bodies could be spotted swaying in the breeze as the wagon headed up the driveway. The hair on the back of Gideon's neck stood on end and a cold chill ran up his back, making him shudder at the sight. Roy and Sissy looked badly discolored and were starting to bloat. From the appearance of their clothes and hair, they had obviously died before the rains. Their hands were tied behind their backs and Sissy's face was contorted into a mask of agony with her eyes still open and bulging.

Doc rubbed his chin as he gazed at the bodies. "May God have mercy on their souls. Those poor people. Sissy wasn't heavy enough to break her neck. She strangled to death," he said as he studied the bodies

Gideon climbed down from the wagon and circled the corpses. "Well, I'd say we have a couple of murders on our hands unless they knew some way to tie their own hands behind their backs."

At that point, Gideon and Doc heard someone running and turned to see Finnie dash behind a tree before heaving.

"Get their bodies down and I'll take a look at them," Doc said.

Waiting until Finnie composed himself, Gideon motioned him over to the bodies. He cut the rope while Finnie secured the cord in his hands and then helped him lower the bodies into the grass as gently as possible. The bodies buckled into macabre positions until the doctor walked over and stretched them out on the ground.

"You two go on and look around or whatever it is that you intend to do and leave me be," Doc said.

They found the cabin undisturbed. Two plates of food sat on the table half eaten and Roy's rifle and shotgun hung on the wall. Rain had washed away any signs of tracks. Gideon trudged back towards the doctor knowing that he had no clues to determine the murderers while Finnie sat down on the porch, not wanting to return to the bodies.

"What can you tell me about things?" Gideon asked as he approached.

"Roy put up a good fight. He has a good deal of bruising all over his body, including his knuckles. Sissy has bruises on her arms where they held her. I don't think she was raped, but she had an absolutely gruesome death," Doc said.

"Roy must not have been suspicious of whoever it was. His guns are still on the wall. They were in the middle of eating and I don't think they were robbed. Nothing looks disturbed. There had to be at least two people to do this," Gideon said.

"I would say so. Roy and Herman Ross had a feud years ago over the open range between their ranches. They both thought that they had a right to it. Sheriff Fuller had to come out to calm things down when Herman threatened to kill Roy. That was a long time ago and I don't know how things were these days," Doc said.

"Let's roll the bodies into the tarps. I hope Finnie can help me lift them into the wagon if they are wrapped," Gideon said.

Doc said, "I guess I can help if he can't. I'd think that Finnie would've seen enough carnage in the war that this kind of thing would not bother him."

"I think seeing this brings all that back to mind. Some things are better off forgotten," Gideon said.

After they had each body rolled into a tarp, Gideon waved at Finnie to join them. The Irishman still looked pale and said little as they lifted the bodies into the wagon and headed back to town. Once there, they left the bodies with the cabinetmaker before Gideon returned the wagon and retrieved the newly shod Buck.

His first order of business involved riding to the edge of town to see the retired Sheriff Fuller. He found the old sheriff out in the yard cleaning fish while puffing on his pipe and blowing smoke plumes like a chimney.

"Gideon Johann, what brings you my way? I bet you came for a fish dinner," Sheriff Fuller said.

"I wish I was. Somebody hanged Roy Weaver and his wife. Doc said that he and Herman Ross had some bad blood. I wanted to see what you thought about it," Gideon said.

Sheriff Fuller removed the pipe from his mouth and placed it on his workbench. "That's a shame. Roy was a pretty good fellow even if he was a little odd. I don't think he and Sissy were ever actually married. Sure hate to hear such terrible news."

"Do you think Herman could have done it? I understand that he threatened Roy. It took more than one person to pull this off," Gideon said.

"That squabble was a good ten years ago. I'd think Herman would have settled that a long time ago if he were going to do it. He just said that in the heat of the argument. I don't think Herman or his boys are capable of being killers. I guess I've seen stranger things happen, but that one would be a shock," Sheriff Fuller said.

"Thanks, I think I'll go have a talk with him just the same. I'd sure come back and have some fish if I'd get an invite," Gideon said, grinning at the old sheriff.

"You know that you're always welcome. You come back here for lunch anytime that you want. I could use the company," Sheriff Fuller said.

Riding back on the same road that he had traveled earlier that day, Gideon rode past the Weaver place down to the Ross homestead. He found Herman sitting on his porch mending tack. The rancher was a tall man and thin as a rail. His long legs and arms seemed to point in all directions as he worked on the leather.

"What brings you all the way out here, Sheriff?" Herman asked as Gideon dismounted.

"Roy Weaver and Sissy were found hanged in their yard. I wanted to know if you saw anything unusual the last few days or know of anybody that might want to kill them," Gideon said and watched the shocked expression come over Herman's face.

"That's terrible. Even Roy didn't deserve that. If you are asking me if I did it, the answer is no," Herman said.

"I understand that you once threatened to kill Roy," Gideon said.

"Sheriff, that was years ago and I said it when Roy and I were in a screaming match. I never meant it and if I were going to kill Roy, I would've done it a long time ago. I'm not going to lie and tell you that we were best friends, but we had gotten to the point where we greeted each other when we crossed paths. We quit fighting over that land and our cattle often grazed together," Herman said.

"What about your boys?" Gideon asked.

Herman stood and color came to his face. "Listen here, Sheriff, my boys wouldn't do nothing like that. Fact is, Roy always treated my boys good even when we were feuding. They wouldn't hurt him or Sissy."

"So you have no idea who would do this?" Gideon said.

"No, sir, I do not. Makes me kind of nervous for the family and me. I'll be looking over my shoulder, that's for sure," Herman said.

"Can I see the back of your hands?" Gideon asked.

Herman held up his hands. They looked red and weather-beaten, but showed no signs of cuts or bruises.

"Keep your eyes open and if you see anything unusual, you come and get me," Gideon said before riding away.

On the ride back to town, Gideon analyzed his conversation with Herman. The rancher seemed genuinely surprised about the murders and sincere in his answers. Based on the rancher's demeanor, he tended to believe that Herman had been telling the truth, but he wasn't ready to mark him off his list of suspects just yet.

# Chapter 7

Smiling with amusement, Mary watched the visitor in the fine suit pause in the doorway of the Last Chance. He stood there looking all around as if he were sizing up the place and trying to decide if it were fit for him to set foot in. Whatever drinking establishments the man had been in previously, she felt sure that he had never visited anything like her saloon. The noonday crowd had thinned out and very few patrons remained. After the stranger seemed to decide that there were no desperados hanging around the place, he cautiously entered and sat down with his back to the wall at the table that Gideon always used.

Mary walked over to him. "Welcome to the Last Stand Last Chance Saloon. What can I get you?"

"I'll have a glass of whiskey," he said in a Boston accent.

"Do you want the stuff that the cowboys around here drink or the good stuff?" Mary asked.

The stranger smiled. "I better have the good stuff. Otherwise, I might begin singing "Buffalo Gals" and make a spectacle of myself."

"We wouldn't want that now, would we?" Mary said.

"Not if you ever heard me sing," he joked.

Mary left to pour the drink and after returning with the whiskey, she said, "May I ask you your name?"

"John. And yours?"

"Mary."

"Would you sit with me if you have the time? I'm trying to learn about Last Stand," John said before rising and pulling a chair out for her.

Mary sat down at the table. "I'm from Indiana originally so I don't know as much as some. From what I understand, settlers came here to raise cattle because of the good grasslands and plenty of water runoff from the mountains. It's a good little town."

"So it is not one of those wild places that we are always reading about back east?" John asked before taking his first sip. "That is pretty good whiskey."

"We're certainly not Dodge City. Not since Gideon came back and became sheriff. Sheriff Fuller got old and things were not being tended to like they should. Gideon cleaned that up, though a couple was just found hanged on their ranch. It's got everybody quite upset," Mary said.

"Really? That seems queer. And nobody has a clue on the murderers?" he said.

"I haven't talked to Gideon about it, but from what I hear, some think it's a neighboring rancher and others say that there is no way that Herman Ross is capable of murder," she said.

"So, Sheriff Gideon is a friend of yours, I take it?" John asked.

"We are friends. He's a good man and we look out for each other. It's good to have the sheriff on your side when you are a woman running a saloon," Mary said.

John chuckled. "Yes, I'm sure that it is."

"Where are you from, John?" she asked.

"Boston," he replied.

"What brings a man all the way from Boston out here to Last Stand, Colorado?" Mary asked.

Smiling and letting out a small sigh, John said, "That's a long story and for another day. I'm the paying customer and I get to ask the questions at least for today."

With her many encounters with men over the years, Mary had developed a keen sense of judging character. She liked John and could spot no malice in the man. There was no doubt much more to his story than he seemed willing to tell, but she didn't see anything sinister in his motives. "What more do you want to know?" she asked.

"Does a town like Last Stand have a doctor?" he asked.

"It does. Doc Abram has been around here forever. In fact, I think he went to medical school in Boston. He likes to pretend to be a grouchy old man, but he's really a sweetheart," Mary said.

"But is he a good doctor?" John asked.

"He's fixed me up a time or two. If you need to see him, don't worry. He's good at what he does," she said.

"I take it that the doctor is also a friend of yours?" he said before taking another drink.

"He is. Some people look down on me for running a saloon and my past, but Doc was never judgmental. He treated me the same as everybody else – which can be a bit brusque at times," Mary said and laughed.

"Well, I can see why you have so many friends. Is your Sheriff Gideon friends with the doctor also?" John said.

"Gideon doesn't have a lot of friends, but Doc is one of them. I think Doc is kind of our stand-in father for us that don't have one," Mary said.

"I see. Doesn't the doctor have his own family?" John inquired.

"No. He's been a bachelor his whole life as far as I know. You sure are curious about Doc and Gideon," she said.

"I'm just trying to learn about some of the pillars of the community. It's been a pleasure talking to you, Mary," John said before tipping his glass and drinking the last of his whiskey and paying her.

Mary watched him walk out of the saloon, carrying himself with command and presence. He certainly piqued her interest and what John from Boston didn't know was that she was determined to figure out why he had arrived in Last Stand.

After putting away the leftover food from lunch, Mary walked to the jail. She found Gideon at his desk and Finnie sitting across from him. Both men seemed distracted and barely gave her a greeting.

Mary plopped down in a chair beside Finnie. "You two aren't very friendly. Makes a girl feel unwelcome."

Gideon ran his hand through his mop of hair. "Sorry, Mary. We're sitting here trying to figure out why Roy and Sissy were hanged and who the murderers might be. We don't have much to go on unless we assume that Herman Ross did it and I don't think that he did. I certainly don't have any evidence to accuse him of doing it."

"You didn't think you were going to solve Minnie Ware's murder either and you did. You'll figure it out," Mary said.

"I hope you're right," Gideon said.

"John, the stranger that came in on the stage, stopped into the Last Chance. We had a nice talk. He's from Boston," Mary said.

Finnie sat up in his chair at the mention of John. "Did you learn anything about him? I looked at the register at the hotel and you couldn't even read his name. He doesn't want anybody to know who he is and I think he's up to no good. It's mighty suspicious that he shows up and two days later, we have two murders. I think we need to talk to him."

Gideon rubbed his cheek and sighed. "This John apparently doesn't know a soul in town. I don't think he committed the murders by himself and I don't know how he would have known where Roy lived or how to get out there. I think you're barking up the wrong tree."

Mary chimed in, "He has hands that are softer than mine. I doubt he's done an ounce of manual labor in life. He doesn't strike me as a killer."

Finnie grabbed the arms of the chair and resituated himself in agitation. "I've been thinking that maybe the killer tied up Sissy when Roy was gone and then waited for him. He could have waylaid him. One person could have done it that way."

Mary chortled. "That might be true, but that still doesn't put John at Roy's place. You think you have it all figured out. I can't see that you're much good in figuring anything out."

Offended, Finnie asked, "What's that supposed to mean?"

"Nothing," Mary replied.

Gideon interrupted the conversation. "I take it that you were impressed with John and I would guess that you used your womanly intuition that you are so proud of to size him up. Did you learn anything about him?" he asked, failing to conceal his disdain for Mary's ability to know what he felt even when he didn't want her to know.

"I do like him, but he doesn't want to talk about himself. He seems like a very nice man to me, but he's here for a reason and I plan to figure it out. He was awfully curious about you and Doc," she said.

"Maybe it was to murder Roy and Sissy," Finnie said, still not willing to let his theory die.

Ignoring Finnie, Mary looked at Gideon and said, "Don't you find it odd that they were hanged instead of shot. Shooting them would have been a lot easier. It's almost like they were handed down sentences and then executed."

"I thought about that too. There's something just not quite right about this whole thing. The pieces don't fit the puzzle. I wonder why this John was asking about Doc and me," Gideon said.

"There seems to be a lot of pieces that don't fit these days," Finnie said.

Gideon let out a sigh and eyed the couple sitting across the desk from him. "You two need to talk to each other and the sooner the better."

# Chapter 8

Having finished the Sunday dinner, Abby and Joann cleared the dishes before joining Gideon and Zack on the porch to watch Winnie and Chance play tag with their dog Red. The children proved no match for the coonhound as he deftly cut and darted from their reach. Chance, only walking for a month, continuously fell on his butt or tripped and landed face first in the yard. Each time he would stand back up, grin, and resume his pursuit of the dog.

"That little fellow sure is determined," Zack remarked.

"He's like his daddy. He's hardheaded," Abby said, smiling at her husband.

Gideon lit his pipe, getting it to burn to his satisfaction, before saying, "It seems to have served me well over the years."

"That's debatable. I'm just now getting you trained proper," Abby said.

Grinning at his wife, Gideon said, "You just like to showoff for Zack and Joann. They know that I got you wrapped around my finger."

Joann waved away the plume of smoke hovering around her head from her father's pipe. "Zack and I are arguing over when to begin building the cabin. I think we should start now and he thinks we should start in the spring. What do you think, Daddy?"

"I tend to agree with Zack. I think that you'll be hard pressed to get a cabin built before winter sets in," Gideon said.

"But you built this place in the fall and got it done, and with the reward money, we can hire to have some of it done for us," Joann said.

"You don't have that money yet and I have no idea how quickly it will come. And you're forgetting that this place already had a well and we were able to reuse the fireplace with only a few repairs. You'd be best to get your well dug this fall before the water levels rise in the spring so you can get it deep enough and then be ready to begin building in the spring. Zack can go ahead and start cutting trees," Gideon said.

Sounding as if she only meant to be half-joking, Joann said, "I should have known that you would agree with him. You always take his side."

"You asked and I told you what I thought. Somebody has to help keep you from running all over him," Gideon said.

"He gets his way plenty. He's not washy like he used to be. In fact, he gets kind of bossy sometimes. I probably should have been happy to leave well enough alone," Joann said.

Zack looked at his wife with bemused affection and shook his head. "Let's take the kids for a walk. I'll carry Chance. He looks about tuckered out," he said and rose from his seat to go pick up his baby brother-in-law.

After they had gone, Abby said, "I've been thinking about that reward money too. With that money, we could expand the ranch and you could resign from being sheriff. Ranching is a lot safer life."

"I thought about that too, but I owe the city council. They appointed me to fill Sheriff Fuller's position when I needed a job and with the understanding that I'd run for the position. I can't resign less than a year after getting elected. And the fact of the matter is that I'd be okay at ranching, but never as good as Ethan, but I'm a pretty darn good sheriff," Gideon said.

"I was afraid you'd say that. I was hoping maybe you were getting tired of people trying to kill you. I know that I am," she said.

"Oh, I'm tired of that part of it, but I think that I help make Last Stand a better place to live. Besides, if I resigned, then Finnie would probably get the job and half the town would never understand what their sheriff was saying with that Irish accent," Gideon said before taking a puff from his pipe.

"I guess you're right, but I like raising cattle. At least Chance is getting big enough that I can put him in the saddle and he can ride with me to check the herd. I miss doing that regularly. We won't have to feel so guilty about hiring help for the herd when we need it either," Abby said.

"No, we won't. We also need to figure out something we want for ourselves and spend some of that money on it. There's no need to hoard all of it," Gideon said.

"I love you, Gideon Johann," she said before sitting in his lap.

"Sure, crawl in my lap when we have company. That doesn't do me any good," he said.

"There's always later," Abby said

"Don't think that I'll forget," Gideon said, grabbing her ass and looking at her grin. He loved the way that her eyes lit up when she smiled and her toothy grin.

"On the subject of Finnie, have you talked to Mary lately?" Abby asked.

"Yeah, I talked to her the other day and if you're hinting at whether I know that she is carrying a child or not – I figured it out all by myself," Gideon said.

"Wow, I'm impressed. Did you give her any advice?" she asked.

"I told her that she needs to talk to Finnie about it. He wants to marry her, but the coward is afraid to ask and I think that he will be thrilled to have a baby. Both of them need to learn to tell the other what's on their mind," he said.

"I hope that you're right. I love Finnie, but I can see why Mary worries about how he will react. He sure can be a hard one to figure out," Abby said.

Abby remained sitting in Gideon's lap as they watched the others return from their walk. Chance slept with his head resting on Zack's shoulder. Winnie, having become possessive of Joann since her sister's marriage, clung to her sibling's hand.

Joann put a hand to her hip. "Well, aren't you two lovey-dovey? You better be careful or somebody might end up with a playmate," she said, nodding her head towards Chance.

"It looks to me like Zack is a natural. Playmates can come from all kinds of places," Abby said.

"Abby," Gideon chided. "We don't need to hear such talk."

Abby and Joann burst into laughter while Zack looked as uncomfortable as Gideon did.

"Daddy, it is a natural thing and it's part of marriage. You can't just pretend that it's not so," Joann said.

"Honey, daddy's can pretend all we want that it ain't so," Gideon said.

Abby climbed out of Gideon's lap.

"Zack, if you would bring Chance into the cabin, we can lay him down," Abby said.

As soon as Abby and Zack disappeared into the cabin, Gideon said, "Winnie doesn't have school Wednesday. When you come over to watch them, do you think you can hitch the wagon and take her and Chance to town to get your picture made? I bought Abby a gold picture locket and I want the three of you in it. Hiram knows about it. Chance likes to ride and will sit in Winnie's lap."

"Sure, I think we can pull that off," Joann answered.

"Winnie, we have to keep this secret. We're going to surprise your momma," Gideon said.

"I can keep a secret," Winnie said.

# Chapter 9

After finishing breakfast in the back room of the saloon, Mary watched as Finnie strapped on his holster and noticed his new revolver. The well-oiled, shiny butt of the gun stood out in sharp contrast to the previous scarred and weather-beaten one that he carried.

You've got a new revolver," Mary remarked.

Finnie looked down at his new gun before gripping it and pulling it out of the holster. "Yeah, I've been saving up for it. I've been fancying Gideon's for a long time and got one just like it. I won't have to carry two sizes of cartridges now. My rifle and it take the same."

"It's very nice as far as guns go. I guess with your new found wealth, you deserve a new gun," she said.

The look on Finnie's face betrayed his surprise and he hesitated before speaking. "I guess you heard about the reward money," Finnie mumbled.

"I did. I would have thought you would want to share such exciting news with me. It's not like I was going to ask you for part of it," she said.

Finnie pulled his shoulders back and straightened his posture. "It's not like you share what you make on the saloon with me," he said defensively.

"That's true, but my income is not nearly as exciting as your reward. We could have celebrated your turn of fortune. It makes me feel as if I'm not that important to you," Mary stated.

"Not that important? What about you? I don't have a clue on how you feel about us," Finnie said, indignation rising in his voice.

"Don't have a clue? Why would you not know how I feel?" Mary said, her voice getting loud.

"Well, do you know how I feel?" he asked.

"I don't know anything anymore," she yelled. Her dark eyes flashing anger.

"And what's the difference then?" Finnie yelled back.

"You thickheaded Irishman. Get out of here before I take that new gun you're so proud of and shoot you with it," Mary hollered.

"Tell me what the difference is. Let's talk about this," Finnie said, his voice somewhat calmer.

"Finnegan Ford, get out of here," she yelled before darting up the stairs to their bedroom.

Grabbing his hat, Finnie pulled it down so hard that it rested against the top of his ears before storming to the jail where he startled Gideon and Doc by slamming the door.

"What's got a burr under your saddle?" Gideon asked.

Finnie related the events that had just transpired before dropping into the seat beside Doc and sinking into it.

"I told you that you should tell her about the reward. You two really need to talk things out," Gideon said.

"Well, obviously you were right, but I did try to talk to her and it got me nowhere," Finnie said.

"Finnie, Mary has as much common sense as any woman that I know, but she's still a woman and they're emotional creatures. I can tell you from experience that when they get like that, you have to wait for them to calm down before trying to reason with them. I don't always follow my own advice, but I should," Gideon said.

"And I gave up the bottle for this," Finnie muttered.

Doc slapped his leg and chortled. "I'm glad I chose the life of a bachelor. You two should hear yourselves. Pathetic."

Finnie glared at the doctor in indignation. The morning had barely begun and he had already about had his fill of people. "Yes, because it would be preferable to grow to be a grumpy old man like yourself. Maybe if you had known the comfort of a woman, you wouldn't be so grouchy."

"If Mary finally tires of that blathering Irish accent and shoots you, I just might let you bleed to death," Doc said.

The Irishman looked at the doctor and then began laughing and rubbing his chin. "You're right. I am pathetic, but so are you."

"Probably true. I guess men and women have been driving each other crazy since Adam and Eve," Doc said.

"Were you their doctor too?" Finnie asked.

The doctor tried not to smile at the Irishman's witticism, but failed.

"Doc, did you ever come close to getting married?" Gideon asked.

The doctor smiled wryly. "Let's just say that if I did, that it was so long ago that I don't remember."

"Well, I hate to break up this party of pathetic men, but Finnie and I are going to ride back out to the Weaver place and have another look around," Gideon said.

Doc took his leave and Finnie left to retrieve his horse from the livery stable. When he returned, he and Gideon rode towards the Weaver ranch. Cooler weather had set in with the coming of September and the leaves were starting to turn. The day made for an enjoyable ride and they never discussed Mary any further, but kept the subjects to the coming winter and guns.

Weaver's place sat undisturbed and looked the same as the last time they were there. The cabin remained as before, lacking both clutter and filth. The lack of a struggle in the house and the half-eaten plates of food on the table still left Gideon believing that the murderers were people that the victims knew. He could see no other way that the couple could've been lured outdoors to their unsuspecting deaths.

"Let's look around outside. There's nothing in here to help," Gideon said.

The two men traipsed around the yard looking as if they were hunting night-crawlers in the daytime. Near the hanging tree, Finnie came to an abrupt stop.

"Gideon, come here," Finnie called out.

Walking over, Gideon spotted the hand carved cross on a leather string that Finnie had found. He bent down and picked up the necklace. The cross measured about three inches long and was crude in workmanship and dark with age. The string looked as if it had been stretched to the point of breaking.

"Finnie, this is very interesting," Gideon said.

"Do you think that it belonged to either Roy or Sissy?" Finnie asked.

"I don't know. I've never heard tell of Roy being a religious man and I don't think Sissy ever converted to Christianity, but I'll ask around and see if anybody knows. Good job in seeing it," Gideon said.

"Well, if it belonged to the killer, he sure had a peculiar way of practicing his religion," Finnie said.

"Exactly," Gideon said. "Let's head back to town."

Once back in town, Gideon spent the rest of the day visiting the town merchants and preachers. Nobody recalled ever seeing Roy or Sissy wearing a cross or attending church, but several people remembered Sissy wearing Indian beads. Gideon stuck the necklace in his desk, more perplexed than when the day had started.

# Chapter 10

Two days after the dustup between Finnie and Mary, Mary remained cool towards him. Her conversations were the minimum necessary to co-exist and he in turn had done his best to avoid her as much as possible. By that night, Finnie decided that it was time to try to get back in Mary's good graces. He walked over to the table where she sat laughing with Doc and John. A couple of trail crews returning south from cattle drives to Kansas were in the Last Chance that night and gave him an excuse to linger in the saloon.

"Care if I join you? I thought I'd keep an eye on all the cowboys," Finnie said.

"Help yourself," Mary said. "I just introduced Doc to John. You might as well be next."

Finnie leaned over the table, shaking John's hand, and introducing himself.

"Good to meet you, Finnie. I'm John. I came all the way from Boston to see your little town."

"You're a far piece from home. What brings you all the way out here?" Finnie asked.

"It's kind of a long story, but let's just say that I have an interest in the west and decided to come see it for myself," John said.

"Did you leave family behind?" Finnie inquired.

Putting her hand upon Finnie's arm, Mary said, "Finnie, quit asking so many questions. I'm sure John will tell us what he wants us to know in good time."

"I don't mind. I did leave my wife and three children back home and I do miss them terribly," John said.

"Doc, didn't you go to school in Boston? It's hard to imagine sitting in Last Stand, Colorado with two men that have ties to Boston. What are the odds of that?" Finnie said.

"I got my medical degree from Harvard. That was a long time ago. I'm sure the town has changed much since then," Doc said.

"The metropolitan area of Boston is over a million people now. It surely is a different place than in my childhood. It's a bit crowded these days," John said.

"A million people. I had no idea. I lost track of anybody from those days a long time ago," Doc said.

"Speaking of ending up in Last Stand, how did you end up here?" John asked.

"Some of the pillars of this community decided that the town needed a doctor and one of them came to Boston to recruit one. I grew up in Pennsylvania and the west always intrigued me so I took them up on their offer," Doc said.

"Did you ever consider staying in Boston?" John asked.

"I did at one time, but I realized that I could never be happy there," Doc answered.

Two men at the bar began arguing. The exchange quickly escalated into a heated altercation with yelling and swearing. Finnie excused himself from the table and walked over to the two cowboys.

"You two need to take a breath and calm down. There's no need for that in here," Finnie said.

The taller of the two men shoved Finnie. "I don't need to be taking orders from some sawed-off deputy. You can go to hell," he screamed.

Finnie regained his balance and sent a right hook crashing into the cowboy's jaw. The man bounced against the bar and then sank to the floor as if lifeless.

Turning to the other cowboy, Finnie showed him his fists. "Would you like to try one of these on for size or can you behave yourself?"

"I'm good. I didn't come here looking for trouble," the man answered.

John watched the disturbance with childlike fascination written on his face. "Did you see that right hook? I've paid to see professional boxing matches and never saw one like that. I really am in the west," he gushed.

"Finnie used to box. He's not to be trifled with," Mary said, failing to conceal her pride in Finnie even if she remained miffed at him.

Looking over to the table, Finnie said, "I shall return." He grabbed the unconscious man by the collar and dragged him out of the salon towards the jail.

"So is Finnie your man?" John asked.

"He is on the good days, but there are times where he comes precariously close to dying at the hands of a saloon owner," Mary said.

"I think that is true for all of us men. We do take some training. Don't you agree, Doc?" John said.

"Don't ask me. I gave up on the female persuasion a long time ago. I would say that I'm an incorrigible bachelor," Doc said.

"Do you have an opinion on the subject, Mary?" John asked.

"I'm a widow. My husband Eugene didn't need any training. He was an easy keeper. Eugene wasn't as funny as Finnie or as much of a character, but he wasn't near the challenge," Mary answered.

"I'm sorry to hear that you became a widow at such a young age," John said.

"How old are you children?" Mary asked, not wanting to dwell on the past.

At the poker table in the back of the saloon, somebody yelled, "You bastard, you're a card cheat." The sound of chairs scooting across the wooden floor echoed across the room as two men stood up from the table. Gunshots rang out as the two card players shot at each from the distance of the tabletop. Black powder clouded the room with smoke and bedlam broke out as people ran and dived in every direction. The gunman with his back to Mary's table fell across the poker table, flipping it over with his weight. The other shooter glanced around the room and then made a run for it across the saloon and out the door.

Finnie heard the gunshots as he locked the door to the cell of his unconscious prisoner. He ran out into the street just as the gunman mounted his horse and came barreling towards him. Attempting to draw his revolver, Finnie forgot that he had begun attaching the holster loop over the hammer of his new Colt. As he looked down to see his problem, the rider crashed into him, sending him somersaulting backwards and sprawling in the street. The sounds of hoof beats faded into the night as he spit dirt and tried to regain his senses.

From the floor of the saloon, Mary and Doc peeked up over the top of the table. They saw John slumped back in his chair. His arms hung to his side and blood gushed from a hole in his chest. He made eye contact with Doc.

"Does this make me a cowboy?" John asked through clenched teeth.

Doc stood and rushed to John's side. "Some of you men get over here and carry this man to my office. What about that one over there?"

"He's dead, Doc," a patron called out.

Four men lifted John and carried him out of the saloon with Doc and Mary following them. Finnie was still crawling around in the street trying to get to his feet. Mary spotted him and ran to his side.

"Finnie, are you shot?" she cried.

"No, I got ran over by somebody's horse. I'm dizzy," Finnie said.

Wrapping her arms around Finnie and hugging him, Mary said, "You crazy Irishman. You scared the hell out of me. I thought I lost my chance to shoot you myself. Let me help you to your feet. John got shot."

With Mary's help, Finnie made it into to the doctor's office and sat down in the doctor's chair. Holding his head in his hands, he sucked in big breaths to clear his head. He still felt woozy as the men that carried John walked past to leave.

The doctor retrieved scissors to begin cutting clothing away. "Is Finnie hurt badly?" he asked.

"He's just shook up. I'm filling him in on what happened," Mary answered.

"Good. Please bring a pen and paper. I need you to do the writing," Doc said.

Mary dug around in the desk drawer before coming over with the writing materials.

Doc leaned down and patted John on the chest. "John, can you hear me?"

"Yes."

"John, I want to be honest with you. You are seriously wounded and may die. I want you to give me your address so that we can notify your family or they may never know what happened to you," Doc said.

"My name is John Hamilton. My wife's name is Kate and I live at 22 Beacon Street. Tell my wife and children that I love them," John whispered.

Doc straightened his posture and looked around the room as if gathering his senses before leaning back over John. "Are you Irene's son?"

"Yes."

Doc took a step back, taking a big breath as if to replenish the air knocked out of him before he exhaled loudly. "Am I your father?" he asked in bewilderment.

John nodded his head and closed his eyes.

Looking up at Mary, Doc rubbed his chin as if he were trying to wear off his whiskers. "I never thought that this day would happen and surely not under these circumstances," he said as much to himself as to Mary.

"Doc, what's going on?" she asked.

"You can help me with the surgery. I'll tell you all about it as we work," he said as he sprang into action.

"I'll do my best," Mary replied.

The doctor walked to his shelf of bottles, pulled the chloroform down, and then retrieved a cloth. "Finnie, how are you feeling?"

"I'm okay now. Just a little stiff. A horse hits harder than I do," Finnie said.

"I would say so. Do you think that you're up to helping hold John down while I chloroform him?" the doctor asked.

"Sure, Doc," Finnie answered as he arose from the chair and gingerly walked over to the table.

With Mary on one side and Finnie on the other, Doc stood at the end of the table by John's head and placed the chloroform soaked cloth over his mouth and nose. John struggled briefly, but he was already barely conscious and weakened to the point that he put up little resistance. Doc held the cloth on John's face until satisfied that his patient would remain sufficiently sedated.

"Go back and rest, Finnie. Thank you for your help," Doc said.

"I need to go back to the saloon and see what I can find out about our shooter before everybody scatters," Finnie said before shuffling out the door.

"What do you want me to do?" Mary asked the doctor as he retrieved his tray of medical instruments.

"Come over here. We're going to scrub our hands and then douse them in carbolic acid. It's a little hard on the skin, but one time shouldn't irritate you too much," he said.

After they sanitized their hands, the doctor wiped the skin around John's bullet hole with the acid and poured some into the wound. "I want you to spray down each instrument that I use with the carbolic acid," he said as he stuck his finger into the wound and began probing. "He's got a fractured rib and I can feel a hole in the lung, but it's on the outer edge. There's the bullet. It's straight back, no ricocheting. Thank goodness it must have missed the subclavian vein or things would really he had. He would bleed out. Hand me the scalpel and forceps, please."

"These things?" Mary asked.

"Yes," the doctor answered and waited as she sprayed the instruments. Doc began grasping the frayed skin around the wound with the forceps and trimming it away with the scalpel. "When I was a student at Harvard, I met Irene Hamilton - a most beautiful creature. Her father was one of the richest bankers in Boston. You can imagine his thrill when his daughter started seeing the son of a dry goods storeowner."

Finished with the trimming, he handed the instruments back to Mary.

"What now?" she asked.

"Hand me the larger forceps after you spray them," Doc answered. He sunk the forceps into John's chest. "They didn't forbid her from seeing me, but they sure didn't like it. I got her pregnant and that's when the real problems began. They made her stop seeing me and she wouldn't even speak to me."

The doctor removed some bone chips from the shattered rib, dropping them into a cup.

"You must have thought about him all the time," Mary said.

"I did in the early years. Over time, I kind of put the whole business on a shelf in the back of my mind. The situation felt hopeless," Doc said. "I got the bullet."

The doctor held the flattened projectile up for Mary to see before dropping it onto the tray.

"I had no idea about all of this, Doc," Mary said.

"No one here does. I've never told a soul in Last Stand. What would be the point? Anyway, after the baby was born, they wouldn't even let me see my own child. I got a scar behind my ear where an officer clipped me with a club to make sure that I got the message. Money can buy lots of things. When I got the chance to come out here, I gave up and left," Doc said as he cleaned the wound again.

"How is John?" Mary asked.

"He's gravely wounded, but I've seen worse and he has a fighting chance. The lung should heal over. We just have to keep things clean. I'm sure he'll want to keep the bullet for a souvenir. It's not every day that you get shot. Do you think he looks like me?" Doc said as he peered at his son's face.

"I was just trying to figure that out. Of course you've been older than the hills since I've known you so I don't know what you once looked like, but I think maybe he does around the eyes," Mary said, trying to lighten the mood.

"It never even occurred to me that he might be my son. I thought that he was an author that had heard about some of Gideon's exploits and didn't want to admit that he was after a story," he said as he began bandaging the wound.

"Don't you need to sew it shut?" she asked.

"No, gunshot wounds heal better if left on their own," he answered.

"Did you ever try writing after you got out here?" Mary inquired.

"I did. I have a whole stack of returned letters stashed away. I had no idea whether or not he even knew my name let alone know where to find me," Doc said.

"He seems like a good man and I don't think that he must bear any ill feelings towards you. He certainly was friendly enough. I think he must have wanted to see what you are like before he told you," Mary said.

"It's all quite perplexing. I'm having a hard time grasping that this man is my son. After all these years, it doesn't seem real to look down and see my own flesh and blood," Doc said and placed his hand on John.

Mary walked over and patted the doctor's back. "This is all terrible, Doc. Every boy should know his father."

"I just hope that he gets the chance to now," Doc said.

# Chapter 11

As Gideon rode through Last Stand towards the jail, he already sensed that something happened the night before. The town didn't feel right as if it were on edge. A raw nervousness remained palpable. He saw Finnie limp out of the saloon headed to the jail.

"What happened?" Gideon called out.

"Oh, Gideon, you are not going to believe it all. The old ladies around here will be singing an opera of gossip when they catch wind of things," Finnie said.

Gideon looked at Finnie with mild annoyance, but decided to wait until they were in the jail to get a real explanation.

"Are you okay?" Gideon asked as he dismounted.

"I'm just stiff and sore. I'm not as young as I used to be. A horse running me down hurts more these days," Finnie said.

"Well, how many times has a horse run you over? I'd think once would be enough to stay out of its way forever," Gideon said.

"It's my first time. That wasn't my point," Finnie said in exasperation before entering the jail and leaving Gideon.

Following him inside, Gideon sat down at his desk. "Tell me what's going on."

"I had to give a cowboy a taste of the old haymaker," Finnie said, holding up his right fist. "While I was locking him up, a gunfight occurred at the poker table. We got a dead cowboy and John from Boston caught a stray bullet. He's hurt bad. I ran into the street and the shooter ran me over with his horse. I guess he's long gone."

"Do you have a name or something?" Gideon asked impatiently.

"Hold on. I haven't gotten to the most shocking part of the night yet. Doc was getting ready to do surgery on John and finds out that John is his son," Finnie said.

Gideon leaned back in his chair with a look of pure astonishment on his face. "What? Did Doc know that he had a son?" he asked in bewilderment.

"I think so. I didn't get all the particulars. Mary did. Our good doctor was pretty shook up," Finnie said.

"I can't believe that old goat never shared with me that he had a son. I'll be damned. Do we have a name or something to find our shooter?" Gideon said.

"His name is Willard Ramsey and he works for the Square Circle Ranch out of El Paso, Texas and grew up down there. His compadres say that he's a good man until he gets to drinking. They also said he's good with a gun and has a stout horse. The latter to which I can attest. Oh, and Blackie reshod his horse yesterday so he should have a sharp distinct track," Finnie said.

"I would guess that John would argue with the claims to his gunmanship. I've seen it happen before and I'll never understand how men standing around a table can miss each other but they can. I'm going to go see Doc," Gideon said and stood.

"Okay, I'll release my cowboy providing he apologizes," Finnie said.

Gideon quietly entered the doctor's office, finding Doc dozing in a chair beside his patient. He gently shook Doc's leg until the doctor awakened.

"Gideon, you missed all the excitement for a change," Doc said.

"So I hear. How's your patient?" Gideon asked.

"He made it through the night just fine. He opens his eyes and mumbles every once in a while, but it's nonsense. He's got a fighting chance," the doctor said.

"How come you never told me that you had a son?" Gideon asked.

"I never thought that I would see him, so what was the point. It was a long time ago and best forgotten. His mother's family wouldn't let me near him. This certainly changes things and I hope I get to hear the whole story," Doc said.

"I'm sure you will, Doc. I'm sure you will. I still can't believe that you have a son. This is about as shocking as me finding out that I had a daughter. There's a lot of secrets in this little town," Gideon said.

"There's lots of secrets in every town. There was a time when the ladies had an eye for me. I wasn't always old you know," Doc said.

"I'm sure you were quite the ladies' man. It looks as if I'll be hitting the trail to find the shooter. I'll see you when I get back," Gideon said.

"You be careful," Doc said, even as his attention drifted to his son.

Gideon walked back to the jail in time to see the cowboy that Finnie had waylaid walk out the door.

"Finnie, I'm going home to tell Abby goodbye. If this Willard Ramsey rode hard, another couple of hours aren't going to make much difference. I'll stop at the Square Circle camp and make sure that he's not hiding there, but I don't hold much hope for that. That would be too easy. You keep an eye on the town and stay out of the way of horses. Did Mary take pity on you and let you back into her good graces?" Gideon said as he grabbed three boxes of cartridges from the ammunition cabinet.

"Pretty much, but not all the way. I sure would've been better off telling her about that reward money. I'm sorry I didn't catch Ramsey and save you from tracking him down. I had the holster loop on my gun's hammer and I messed up," Finnie said.

"It was just bad timing that you were at the jail. You would've had to make one hell of shot to hit him anyway with him barreling down on you. I just hope I don't have to chase him all the way back to Texas. I always swore that I'd never set foot in that place again. I'll see you when I get back," Gideon said and grabbed his slicker off the peg as he headed out the door.

Abby took the news of Gideon's departure about as he expected. She was not pleased and reminded him that chasing outlaws provided one more reason to give up the sheriff business. He did his best to pacify his wife before leaving her and Chance with one last hug.

The camp of the Square Circle proved easy enough to find and the trail boss a pleasant man. Gideon learned that Ramsey returned to camp the previous night to retrieve some belongings and hastily departed before the trail boss knew what had happened back in town. Once again, Gideon was warned of Ramsey's prowess with a gun, especially a rifle, and his unpredictable nature when drinking. The wanted cowboy had been last seen leaving camp headed southeast.

Gideon picked up the track outside of the camp and followed them. The news shoes and the pace of Ramsey's horse made it easy to distinguish the tracks from others. The cowboy had put his horse in an easy lope with the obvious attempt to cover a lot of miles without wearing down his horse. After riding a couple of hours, Gideon was surprised that the cowboy's path headed towards Santa Fe instead of the Goodnight-Loving Trail. Ramsey had opted for the seclusion of the mountains over the ease of the cattle trail.

The September day was cool and sunny, making for the kind of trip that Gideon preferred. With no concerns for overheating his horse, Gideon pushed the pace. He was familiar with the trail, having traveled the path a couple of times in the last few years. Every few miles he would check for tracks to make sure that Ramsey had not veered from the trail.

After a few hours of riding, he came upon grasslands yellowed from lack of rain. Some of the creeks had gone dry from an absence of mountain runoff and the streams looked half the size of their normal flow. The rainfall had been scarce enough that even the trees looked to have suffered from the drought. The pine groves stood carpeted in shed needles deeper than Gideon had ever witnessed.

Towards nightfall, Gideon came to a stream and found signs that Ramsey had made camp there. The remnants of a fire felt cool to the touch and Gideon realized that he probably had not made up any ground on the cowboy. He was dealing with a good horseman intent on escaping. Tired from riding, and with belly growling, he decided to call it a day. Before starting a fire, he unsaddled Buck and tied him so that he could drink from the stream and graze on grass still green from the moisture provided by the water. Dining on hardtack and jerky, he washed the food down with water and a nightcap of a couple sips of whiskey before turning in for the night.

In the morning, Gideon awoke cold and stiff. The morning air hung cold and heavy, and he didn't want to waste time making a fire. He took a sip of whiskey to knock the chill off and decided to skip breakfast rather than face another piece of hardtack. Stretching his limbs, he loosened his muscles to the point where he didn't feel as if he would break in two while riding. With Buck saddled, he rode out as first light turned the landscape to a dull gray.

The farther south he rode, the scraggier the landscape became. The grass thinned out to scrub brush broken up by the occasional pine grove at the foot of the bare mountains. As noontime neared, Gideon came to the lake where the year before he found his old scouting partner, Farting Jack Dolan. He was surprised and tickled to see the tepee still standing, having assumed that Jack would have moved on by now.

"Farting Jack, it's Gideon. Can you hear me?" Gideon shouted as he rode towards the tepee.

The flap of the tepee flew back, and Farting Jack stepped out decked in a new deer hide wardrobe. His steel-gray hair and beard looked to have grown another six inches since Gideon last laid eyes upon him and he remained as skinny as ever.

"Gideon Johann, you old dog. Good to see you again. You just can't stay away from me," Jack said.

"I guess not. You're looking good in your new deer hides. I didn't think that I'd still find you here," Gideon said.

"I tanned me some hides this summer. I never planned to stay, but never came up with a reason to leave and I keep my belly full. I was just getting ready to fry some fish. Stay to eat?" Jack said.

"I surely would. I skipped breakfast. I've eaten about a lifetime of hardtack and it's getting tough to take," Gideon said.

"Well, climb down and catch me up on the news," Jack said as he threw some wood onto his fire.

"I'm chasing a cowboy that killed a man over a poker game and seriously injured a bystander. Have you seen anybody?" Gideon said as he squatted by the fire.

"Saw one around suppertime yesterday. You're a far piece behind him if he's your man," Jack said as he dropped the fish into his skillet.

"That I am. I would imagine that's him. He's got to slow his pace or he's going to wear down his horse. He'll stop eventually," Gideon said.

"They always do. We always got our man back in the day, didn't we?" Jack said.

"That we did. Why don't you ride with me? You can keep me company. It would do you good," Gideon said as he inhaled the smell of cooking fish.

"I just might. I'm set for the winter and got nothing that needs doing," Jack said before turning the fish over in the pan.

With the fish fried, they began eating their meal. Gideon did most of the talking while they ate, telling Jack about Abby, Joann, and Chance. Jack, preoccupied with the fish, grunted occasionally as Gideon unveiled his life in Last Stand.

Gideon took his last bite and said, "So, are you going with me or not?"

"I believe I will. I think I can handle your chattiness. You've talked more today than I remember in all our times together. That dark cloud that hung over you is all sunshine these days," Jack said.

"I suppose so. It's amazing what a good woman and friends can do for you," Gideon said.

Jack retreated to the tepee, gathering his gear, before fetching his horse. As he mounted the animal, he let out an eruption of nauseous gas. Gideon's horse pinned his ears back and backed away from the other horse.

"Buck still remembers you," Gideon said with a laugh.

"Whoa, that was a good one," Farting Jack said before they rode away.

# Chapter 12

Awakening from his first good sleep since the shooting, Doc climbed out of his bed and went immediately to check on his patient. The doctor remained concerned that John Hamilton continued to run a low-grade fever since the shooting even though the wound appeared to be healing well. His patient had barely spoken and was sometimes incoherent when he did. Doc found John propped up in bed using the headboard as a backrest and smiling as the doctor entered the room. His son still looked pale and his eyes remained dark and sunken, betraying that he still remained ill, but he looked his best since the shooting.

"You must be feeling better," Doc said.

"I do. I doubt I'll be dancing today, but I think I could sing a tune," John said.

"That's good to hear. You've been seriously wounded. You'll need time to heal," the doctor said.

"I guess I'll have quite the story to tell when I go back east. I'll have to lie and say that Jesse James shot me – make the story considerably more interesting," John said.

"Yes, that would sound substantially better than a drunk cowboy missing another man standing five feet away and hitting you," Doc said, rubbing the sleep from his eyes.

"I suppose you have a lot of questions for me?" John asked.

"I do, but I can wait until you're ready. After all these years, a few more days won't make much difference," Doc said.

"I think I could eat a horse. If you could get us some food, I think I feel up to talking," John said.

"I'll do it," Doc said.

The doctor threw some kindling into his stove and got the coffee cooking before changing into his normal attire. He walked to the hotel in a lively step and ordered two plates of eggs, bacon, and biscuits with gravy. Returning to his office just as the coffee finished brewing, he poured two cups and sat down with his son to eat.

"Our first meal together. It only took forty-five years and a few odd months," John said.

"So it would seem," Doc said and sipped his coffee.

John took a bite of eggs, closing his eyes and concentrating on the taste. "Oh, my God, this tastes good. I'm about starved."

"You should be. I wasn't able to get much down you. An appetite is a good sign," Doc said as he marveled at his son's attack on the plate of food.

"Mother never married and I've lived my whole life in my grandparent's house. They both died several years ago before I married Kate. We lived with Mother. She died in January," John said.

Doc leaned back in his chair, rubbing his chin. A pained expression came over his face and he briefly got lost in a memory. "I'm sorry for your loss and to hear that. She was a fine woman."

"No one would ever tell me anything about you. You were a taboo subject and my imagination ran wild. I had you being everything from a rapist to the president

LAST RIDE • 77

of the United States," John said and sighed. "Mother knew that she was dying and told me about you on her deathbed."

"Not that it matters now, but I didn't want things to turn out the way that they did. As I'm sure that you know, your grandfather was quite the domineering man and he wanted no part of me marrying your mother," Doc said between bites of bacon.

"Yes, he was, and Mother told me that he forbid you from seeing her or me. I'm sure he thought that Mother would marry some Boston Brahmin in due time. It did not turn out that way," John said.

"You seem to have turned out just fine," Doc remarked.

"I suppose so, but there were times that a father would have been nice. Did you ever try to see me in later years?" John said.

"I have a whole stack of letters that were returned unopened. I almost went back when you would have been about eighteen, but Last Stand had an influenza outbreak and by the time it had past, I lost my will to go," Doc said.

"I'm sorry that I didn't tell you who I was right from the beginning, but I wanted to get a sense of you before you knew I was your son. Besides, I was scared to death to tell you," John said.

"Not an everyday conversation for sure," Doc said.

"Mother insisted that I come to meet you. I'm not sure why it took her dying to decide I should know about my father and that we should meet. I guess maybe she wanted to provide me with a parent after she was gone. The really sad part was that she wanted me to tell you that pushing you away was the mistake of her life and she wished that she could live it all over again," John said.

Doc set his fork down and pressed his fist against his lips as he inhaled a big breath of air. His appetite had vanished and he felt queasy. "That's the thing about life, isn't it? We seldom get to rectify our mistakes until it becomes too late."

"Are you sorry that I came?" John asked.

"Good gracious, no. Now is better than never. Tell me about you and your family," Doc said.

"I've taken over the family banking business. Granddad groomed me for that my entire life. By the time that I was sixteen, I knew more about banking that most men do coming out of college. Kate is my wife. She was not happy with this trip, but she understood. Wait until she finds out that I got shot. She's a wonderful person. I have three children – Henry is sixteen, Rose is thirteen, and Tad is three. I can tell you more later. My belly is full and all I want to do is sleep," John said.

"You get some rest. It sounds as if you have a wonderful family," Doc said before walking out of his office. A sense of gratitude overwhelmed him for having just experienced his first conversation with his son, but for some reason, he felt more alone than he had in years. As he walked towards the alley behind the Last Chance, he quickly realized that the source of his melancholy was the knowledge of what might have been with John's mother and that now never could be.

Doc entered the Last Chance through the back door and found Mary standing over a wash pan on the table. She made retching sounds and looked pale.

"Mary, are you sick?" the doctor asked.

"You could say that," Mary managed to say between heaves.

"Oh, my goodness, you're with child. Why didn't you tell me?" Doc said.

Waving the doctor off with her hand, she said nothing until the last wave of the nausea had past. "I wasn't ready to tell you."

"I'm surprised that big mouth Irishman didn't tell me. I bet he's excited," Doc said.

"He doesn't know. I haven't told him yet either," Mary said as she sat down in a chair. The dry heaves seemed to have robbed her of all her energy.

"Mary, he needs to know. You're going to have to lead that horse to water and pour the water down his throat. He's too scared of the answer to ask you to marry him," Doc said.

"How do you think I feel? I wonder if he really plans to stay with me and that maybe a baby will send him on his way," Mary said.

"I don't think that for a minute. I think you will make him a very happy man. And besides, you can't keep it a secret forever so you might as well tell him and get it over with. Quit making yourself miserable. You're the toughest woman I've ever known. Don't go getting soft on me now," he said, sitting down beside her and putting his hand on her arm.

A small laugh escaped her and she wiped the moisture from her eyes. "I probably should have become an old maid, providing an old whore can be such a thing. How's John?"

"He's much improved. We ate breakfast together and talked. I'll tell you about it later. Why don't you march yourself down to the jail and get this burden off your chest. I'll walk you down there," Doc said.

"You think I should?" she asked.

"I do. Let's go," he said and helped her to her feet before she had too much time to think.

Doc walked Mary to the jail door, encouraging her all the way.

"Go in there and tell him," Doc said before crossing the street to his office.

She hesitated at the door before charging in and finding Finnie sitting at Gideon's desk with his feet on its top, wanted posters in his lap, and puffing on a cigar that had the room filled with smoke.

"I guess when the cat's away, his mouse will play," Mary said.

Putting his feet on the floor, Finnie asked, "Mary, what brings you over?"

Sitting down across from him, Mary waved the smoke away from her face. "We need to talk."

"Okay, what's on your mind?" Finnie asked as he set the posters down and scooted his chair closer to the desk.

Mary took a big breath of the reeking air and exhaled slowly. "Finnie, we're going to have a baby."

"We are?" he said. His face betrayed neither excitement nor disappointment, but only astonishment and he took a puff on the cigar.

"That's all that you have to say?" Mary asked.

"I'm just surprised. How did that happen?" he asked in his stupor.

"How do you think it happened? With the life that I've lived, I assure you that I'm not the biblical Mary," she said.

Finnie managed a small chuckle. "I know that. A baby is something that you've never talked about and I figured that you couldn't have children. I never brought it up for fear of upsetting you."

"Well, I didn't think that I could, but I guess we know differently now. Are you sorry that I'm with child?" Mary said.

"No. No, not at all. It's just that this is the most surprising thing that you could've ever told me. I guess we should get married," Finnie said.

Mary straightened herself up in the chair and her face grew stern. "You guess? I don't want to wed a man that guesses we should get married. I want somebody that knows that he wants to marry me. Finnegan Ford, you couldn't say the right things these days if your life depended on it. At least when you were a drunk you had an excuse for some of your behavior. Well, I'm raising this child for better or worse no matter how you feel about our baby or me. I think you need to sleep over here," she said before standing and walking out the door, slamming it so hard that Finnie feared it would come off the hinges.

He stared at the door long after she had gone and wondered how their exchange had gone so wrong. He knew he could have chosen his words better, but it seemed to him that Mary had been a mite bit touchy about the whole thing. Taking a big puff on the cigar, he sunk into the chair feeling defeated even though the thought of a child elated him.

# Chapter 13

The pursuit of Willard Ramsey proved to be more of a daunting task than Gideon expected. From the looks of the tracks that Ramsey's horse left, he and Farting Jack were not gaining ground on the criminal. They pushed their horses as hard as they dared in the sparse land, but Ramsey appeared headed back to El Paso as quickly as possible.

Spending time again with Farting Jack provided company on the tedious all day rides. Gideon told Jack about all the changes in his life and the old trapper entertained with his tales of long ago escapades of trapping beaver and trading with the Indians. Some of the stories Jack told, Gideon had heard at least a dozen times, but laughed at them nonetheless. Jack knew how to spin a yarn.

They were sitting around the campfire and Gideon asked, "Jack, do you ever have any regrets for the life that you've lived?"

Jack blew a plume from his pipe, looking into the cloud of smoke as if searching for an answer, and then raised his hip and farted. "Not a one. Do you realize the adventures I've lived? I've experienced things that are never going to be again. I've known Indians that were my friends, had ones that tried to kill me, and I've killed my share in battle. I suppose that all of them were honorable people in their own way. I've seen buffalo herds that went on for miles. You could feel the ground shake as they passed. I've never seen a more majestic beast. By the time that your son reaches your age, there won't be any Indians or buffalo left. They'll just be memories. Life is still hard out here, but it's nothing like it used to be and I was a part of all of it. I never got along much with women anyways and I never had the patience for kids, so I have no regrets there. A whore served me just fine when I had the need. I've spent a lot of time alone, but that's the way I liked it. No, I can't say that I have any regrets. It's been a good life," he said before taking a draw on his pipe.

"It certainly has. I'm sure glad that we crossed paths," Gideon said.

"What about you? You got any regrets?" Jack asked.

"I'll always regret killing that little boy and all the years I wasted running from myself. You don't ever quit regretting things like that even if the shooting was an accident. You can never fix it and it eats away at you. Coming back to Last Stand taught me how to get past it, but I'll never be over it. When I get to feeling low, I start thinking about the life that little boy never got to have," Gideon said.

"All wars are good for is getting the wrong people killed. They should've never allowed slavery in the first place. What kind of man thinks that he can own another? Killing that boy lays at the feet of a lot more people than just you who pulled the trigger. You're a good man, Gideon. One of the few that didn't try my patience – at least most of the time," Jack said and belly laughed.

"I think I'm going to turn in. I'm afraid we're going have to chase that son of a bitch all the way to El Paso," Gideon said as he stretched out.

"Well, by God, we can do it. Good night," Jack said before lying down.

They arose early the next morning and hit the trail, arriving in Santa Fe at a little after one o'clock in the afternoon. Gideon had been to the town before, but this was Jack's first visit. As they rode through the central plaza, the old trapper spun in all directions as he took in the sights of the adobe structures and the Palace of the Governors. They came to the sheriff's office and Gideon walked inside the building. The jail was empty and he waited until the sheriff arrived a few minutes later.

"Sheriff, I'm Gideon Johann. I'm the sheriff of Last Stand, Colorado," Gideon said.

"You're a far piece from home. I don't suppose this is a social visit," the sheriff said as he extended his hand.

Gideon shook it. "We tracked a man named Willard Ramsey here. He killed one man and seriously wounded another in a poker game. I wanted to see if you had come across him and also let you know that we were in town before we begin looking for him."

The sheriff sat down at his desk. "If you had got here about an hour ago, I could have made things a lot easier for you. He got in a fight yesterday and I locked him up overnight. I ran him out of town about an hour ago. I'm sorry. I wish I had known."

"Damn, just my luck. Well, we're a lot closer than we were. With a little luck, I'll have him before nightfall," Gideon said.

"I wish you luck. He seems to be a mean one. I had to lay him upside the head with my revolver. You be careful," the sheriff said.

"Thank you, Sheriff. I intend to be," Gideon said before leaving.

Heading south of Santa Fe, the land turned even more barren with very little vegetation. The terrain was hilly and cut by steep-sided gulches and arroyos that they had to wind around as they trailed Ramsey. The land looked so bleak that Gideon felt lonesome just looking at it. Water would be scarce, and searching it out a necessity if the trip continued for days.

After riding for a couple of hours at a trot for most of that time, Gideon and Jack came around a big hill and saw a man they presumed to be Willard Ramsey watering his horse in a small creek. The man saw them at the same time and quickly jumped up, using his horse as a shield. He disappeared up a gully coming off the hill.

"This is not good," Gideon said as they looked for cover before turning around to get behind the hill.

"What now?" Jack asked as they brought the horses to a stop.

"I wish we had an idea what that gulch looks like. He might be able to climb the wall of that thing and shoot us from here. I'll climb the hill and see if I can get a drop on him," Gideon said.

The hill presented a steep climb for Gideon, his boots finding poor footing navigating the surface, and provided very little protection except for a few crops of rock. He had climbed about three quarters of the way up the hill when he saw Ramsey's head and rifle pop up out of the gully not thirty yards away. Gideon hurled himself behind a small ledge of rocks as the first shot kicked up dirt. The rock outcrop was so small that it forced him to lie flat to keep from exposing himself and every time he tried to peek out, he was greeted with a bullet spinning his direction.

"Can you see him? He's got me pinned down," Gideon hollered to Jack.

"No, there's too much curve to the hill," Jack answered.

"Damn, I may have to wait until dark to get out of this mess," Gideon yelled back.

"To hell with this. I'm tired of tracking his sorry ass," Jack said as he pulled his rifle from the scabbard and put his heels to his horse.

Jack rounded the hill and charged up the gully, aiming his rifle at Ramsey as he rode. In his peripheral vision, Ramsey caught sight of Jack and spun to face him. The two men started shooting at each other as fast as they could cock their rifles.

Gideon listened to the ensuing war until complete silence abruptly fell upon the land. He called out to Jack, but received no reply. Peeking his head over the rock, he saw no sign of Ramsey. Panic made his heart race and Gideon ran to the edge of the ravine with his revolver drawn. He saw Ramsey lying sprawled down at the bottom of the gully and Jack slumped over his horse. Crawling over the edge, Gideon walked and slid to the bottom of the gulch. He flipped the lifeless body of Ramsey over and spotted a bullet hole in the outlaw's forehead. Running to Jack, the old trapper sat up in the saddle. His chest was drenched in blood and each beat of his heart squirted out more.

"Did I kill the son of a bitch?' Jack asked.

"He's dead. Jack, let's get you off that horse. You're hurt bad," Gideon said.

"No, you'll never get me back in the saddle and I don't want to be buried in this godawful place. Would you bury me by that lake where I've been living? Would you do that for me, Gideon?" Jack said.

"Jack, we've got to get you to a doctor," Gideon said as his hope began to fade with each squirt of blood from Jack's chest.

"Gideon, you're a good boy. I always liked you and you always did right by me. I can't think of anybody that I'd rather have been with on my last ride. You can have all my possessions. Do I have your word on my burial?" Jack said.

Gideon reached up and took Jack's blood covered hand. "You have my word. Jack, I'm sorry I got you into this mess. I should have handled this myself."

Jack began slowly slumping in the saddle. "Nothing to be sorry for. I came because I wanted to. A man needs an adventure every now and then to know that he's really alive. I'd rather die this way than freeze to death some winter because I got too old to take care of myself. You can tell a story about Farting Jack Dolan every once in a while so that my memory can live on, okay?" he whispered.

"I'll do it. You go trap you some beaver and keep me a place warm at the campfire," Gideon said as Jack draped over the horse's neck.

Realizing that Jack was gone, Gideon turned and kicked a rock. He tried fighting back the tears, but the last couple of years had changed him into a man that no longer possessed the stoicism to hold them at bay. Jack was the first person in a long time that Gideon had been close to that had died and the loss overwhelmed him to the point of having to sit down on the ground and collect himself. Guilt soon replaced the mourning. He chastised himself for having ever asked Jack to come along and lamented the fact that sometimes the most seemingly inconsequential decision could have such drastic outcomes.

Once he regained his composure, Gideon tied Jack onto his saddle. He couldn't lift Ramsey onto his horse so he covered him in rocks where he fell. Stringing the horses together, he started on his journey back to Santa Fe.

Dusk was settling onto the town by the time Gideon reached the sheriff's office. The sheriff helped him get Jack's body off the horse and sent a deputy to get a tarp. They wrapped Jack in it and then tied him across the saddle. The sheriff tried to persuade Gideon to stay the night, even offering his home, but Gideon wanted only to ride. He gave Ramsey's horse and guns to the sheriff, thanked him, and rode away with his mind in a stupor.

He pushed himself and Buck as hard as he dared on the trip back to the lake. He occasionally stopped for a couple of hours to nap and maybe eat before again pushing on down the trail. Both he and his horse were thinner from the pace, but Gideon had little appetite. Burying Jack and getting home were all that he cared about.

Having arrived at the lake at sunrise, he found a shovel in the tepee and began digging the grave by the lakeside. The soil was soft and he made good time on digging the hole. Fatigue had set in to the point that Gideon could barely think, but he refused to rest until satisfied that the grave was suitable for burying Jack. He pulled the body down from the horse and rolled Jack into the grave.

"Jack, I hope we meet up again someday. I believe we will. You were a good one and you taught me a lot.

Happy trapping," Gideon said and began shoveling dirt into the hole.

After filling the hole, Gideon intended to make a grave marker, but he staggered with exhaustion walking towards the horses to unsaddle them and realized that he couldn't push any further. He turned the horses loose and crawled into the tepee. Sleep overcame him within minutes.

When Gideon awoke, the sun was getting low in the west. He grabbed Jack's fishing pole and the worms that he had saved while digging the grave and walked down to the lake. The fish were apparently as hungry as he was and he caught a couple within a half-hour. By the time he cleaned them and had a fire burning, darkness was settling in. The fish tasted about as good as any food he had had in his life, and with his belly full, he felt like a living person again. He retrieved a bar of soap from his saddlebag, stripped down naked, and walked into the lake. The water was cold and he cursed loudly before plunging completely in. As he scrubbed, the rough soap felt good against his skin as if he were peeling off layers of dirt, and he began to sing. After washing his hair, he scampered to the fire to dry before dressing. With nobody to talk with and nothing to do, he went back to the tepee and fell asleep.

He slept through the night. In the morning, he fashioned a crude cross from a couple of tree branches and bound them with a strip of leather. He carved Jack's name into the wood the best that he could with his knife and planted the cross into the ground. Giving his work one final look, he walked back to the tepee. Jack was a man of very few possessions. Gideon kept the old trapper's knife, guns, and a deerskin coat with beadwork that Jack bought years ago from a Ute squaw. The coat fit so he left it on. He inhaled the scent of the jacket, a combination of leather and pipe smoke, and felt better about leaving Jack.

After saddling the horses, Gideon rode off thinking about Farting Jack Dolan. The old trapper would be forgotten in another generation even though he had played a part in the settling of Colorado. Jack certainly was the finest tracker Gideon had known and the only loner he had ever come across that liked to talk a blue streak when in company. Gideon knew that he had had the honor of knowing a man that died a true original and he felt the loss keenly. He smelled the jacket again and tried to focus on getting home to his family.

# Chapter 14

Gideon finally arrived back in Last Stand in the afternoon and found Doc, John Hamilton, and Finnie sitting in front of the jail. John had felt well enough to leave the doctor's office for the first time that day and sat beside his father on the bench. Finnie sat in a chair, leaning back against the wall on two legs, looking the picture of contentment.

Eyeing the three men with begrudging admiration, Gideon said, "Good to see that the town is in such fine shape that the deputy and the doctor can rest on their laurels and asses in front of my jail. How have things been?"

"Well, hello to you too. The town's been quiet since you left if you don't count Mary on the warpath. When I learned I have a child on the way, I somehow made a mess of it," Finnie said.

"Imagine that," Gideon replied sarcastically.

"Isn't that Farting Jack's horse?" Finnie said, ignoring the mockery.

"It is. He died helping me catch Ramsey. I don't feel like talking about it right now. In fact, I don't feel like talking at all. I just want to go home to cleanup and see my wife and kids," Gideon said.

"I'm sorry to hear that, Gideon," Finnie said.

"John, I'm glad to see that you're up and getting around," Gideon said before nudging Buck into a walk.

As Gideon disappeared down the street, Doc turned to Finnie and said, "I take it that Mary hasn't calmed down from your blunder?"

"No, I'm still sleeping on the cot in the jail. She won't even talk to me. That woman may be an orphan and have no idea about her family, but I can assure you she has Irish in her. Only an Irish woman can stay mad as long as she does," Finnie said.

"Or maybe it takes an Irishman to infuriate a woman so badly that they stay mad no matter their heritage," Doc said.

Finnie chuckled and said, "You may have a point there. We do seem to be a troublesome bunch. Have you talked to her?"

"I've talked to her, but when I brought up your name, she cut me off like a hatchet on the poor chicken's neck," Doc said.

Finnie leaned over and looked at John. "Since you seem to be the only one of us here that has successfully navigated the slippery slope of courting a woman, do you have any advice?"

"I find that the phrase 'Yes, dear' goes a long ways in solving most problems," John said.

The three men exploded into laughter. Finnie slapped his leg and the motion caused the reclining chair to slide out from under him, sending him crashing down onto the sidewalk to the chorus of more laughter.

As Finnie stood, he said, "I don't know why I act like this is so funny. If I don't get Mary to come around, I don't know what I'm going to do."

"Give her some time. She'll come around, but you have to handle things better when you get your chance," Doc said.

"I surely hope so," Finnie said as he dusted off.

"Speaking of your wife, you haven't told me much about her," Doc remarked.

John's face lit up. "Kate was a waitress at this café that all of us Harvard boys liked to frequent. We all had quite the high opinion of ourselves and Kate would skewer us like a pig on a spit. I found it absolutely charming. I'd been told all my life how our family wasn't like the common laborers and that it was best to be with our own kind. I expected quite the row when I told Mother that I was seeing her, but she never once said anything disparaging. She and Mother grew to be quite close. Of course Grandfather had passed by then. He would have had a conniption fit if he were still living. Anyway, we are quite happy."

"There seems to be a lot of women that like to skewer men. Abby and Sarah both keep Gideon and Ethan on their toes too. And poor old Zack, I feel for him," Finnie said.

"It's because you all like challenging women. It's not a coincidence. There's plenty of demure women. You all just aren't interested in them," Doc said.

"For a lifelong bachelor, you sure think that you know a lot about women," Finnie said.

"A lot can be learned by sitting back and watching all you fools," Doc reminded him.

"How about I tell you about my children," John said to change the subject. "Henry, being the oldest, is too serious for his own good and he is smart. I believe that he'll go far. Rose is the bossy one of the bunch. She's smart too and rules the roost. And then there's Tad. He came along after we thought we were done with all that nonsense of raising children. I swear I believe that he could turn out to be an outlaw. Everybody has coddled him far too much, I fear."

"It sounds as if you have a nice family, John. I hope I get to meet them someday," Doc said.

"Oh, I insist. We need to get to know each other and plan for it," John said.

Melancholy settled over Finnie. "I hope that I get to know my own child. Mary may kill me before it's born."

∞

Winnie and Chance played in the yard as Gideon rode up to the cabin. Chance began crying and Winnie let out a shriek at seeing the scruffy bearded man in the deer skinned coat.

"It's me, your daddy," Gideon said as he climbed down from Buck.

Abby came flying out of the cabin at the sound of her children and saw her husband standing by the horses. "Thank God, you're back. I've been worried sick about you. I didn't think you'd be gone so long," she said as she walked to Gideon and hugged him.

"It's been a long trip for sure and not a good one," Gideon said as he scooped up Chance. The child stopped crying after hearing his father's voice and held out his hands to touch Gideon's beard. Gideon put his hand on Winnie's shoulder and walked to the porch where he sat down on the swing.

"So what happened and where did you get that jacket?" Abby asked as she sat beside her husband.

Gideon filled his wife in all that had transpired on the trip and how he came into his new possessions.

"I'm sorry, Gideon. I know that Jack meant a lot to you," she said.

"I never should've asked him to go with me. I got him killed," he said.

"Honey, Jack doesn't sound like the type of man that did anything that he didn't want to do. I'm sure he was lonely and enjoyed the company. He had to know the danger. You were just being a friend," Abby said.

"I'd hate to be my enemy then," Gideon remarked.

"Gideon, stop it. You've been down this path before and nobody knows better than you that guilt gets you nowhere. His death is unfortunate, but you didn't cause it. Please stop. You scare me when you get like this," Abby pleaded.

Gideon wrapped his arm around his wife and pulled her against him. "I'll try, but it's hard letting him go. They don't make men like Jack anymore. He was an original."

"You know that if you'd give up this sheriffing business, you wouldn't have to deal with things like Jack getting killed," Abby said.

"We've already been over this. It's what I'm good at doing. Besides, I'd have to worry about Finnie being all on his own if I quit," Gideon said.

"What about the children and me if something happens to you?" Abby asked.

"Nothing is going to happen to me and with the reward money and your money, you'd probably have a line of suitors waiting at your door before I got good and cold," Gideon said, poking her in the ribs and making her smile.

"You need to take a bath and shave. You smell like a goat," Abby teased.

"I think I'm going to leave my mustache. I haven't worn one in years," Gideon said.

"Not if you're planning on kissing me. I can kiss the dog if I want to feel whiskers. I like my man's face to feel like a baby's butt," Abby said.

Gideon cackled. "I'm not sure that's the image I want my wife to have when she's kissing me."

# Chapter 15

Early morning light washed over the town, turning the interior of the jail into a shadowy gray. Finnie opened his eyes and stared at the ceiling as he tried to will himself awake. He sensed someone watching him even though he had not heard the bell above the door ring. Once before he had been waylaid in the jail and his heartbeat quickened. His holster hung beside him and he made a grab for his revolver. As he sat up, he could see the silhouette of someone standing by the desk.

"Don't shoot me. I don't have a gun," a girl's voice called out.

"Move over by the door," Finnie ordered.

He waited until the girl moved before striking a match and lighting an oil lamp. Standing before Finnie was a girl that looked to be in her teens. She stood a little taller than average and rawboned, giving her arms and legs the appearance of being unusually long. Clothed in a worn out dress, the garment did nothing for her already plain features. Her feet were bare and her arms and legs showed scratches as if she had run through a briar batch.

"What are you doing in here?" Finnie asked.

"I need to see the sheriff," the girl answered.

"I'm Deputy Finnegan Ford. You can talk to me," Finnie said.

"I know who you are. You live in sin at the saloon with that whore. I'll wait for the sheriff," she said matter-of-factly.

"Watch your mouth, young lady. There's no need for talk like that. What's your name?" Finnie said.

"Charlotte Bell," she answered.

"Well, have a seat, Charlotte. The sheriff will be here directly," Finnie said before beginning the process of making coffee.

Gideon walked into the jail an hour later to find Charlotte and Finnie sitting in chairs facing his desk. Finnie sipped coffee and looked agitated.

"What's going on?" Gideon asked as he eyed the girl suspiciously and wondered what his first day back at the jail would be like.

"This is Charlotte Bell. She is here to see you and refuses to tell me her reasons for being here," Finnie said brusquely.

Sitting down at his desk, Gideon asked, "So what can I do for you, Charlotte?"

"My family lives at Paradise. Old Pastor Gordon died a few months back and now young Pastor Gordon has taken over. He's arranging marriages for everybody sixteen and over that's still unmarried. I'm supposed to marry Cecil Hobbs this week and I can't stand to even look at that odd fish. Pastor Gordon carries on about the sin of fornication all the time. Well, I ain't fornicating and I ain't going to do my wifely duties if it's with Cecil Hobbs either. You have to protect me. They'll be coming," Charlotte said.

Gideon leaned back in his chair and felt a knot forming in his stomach. He had never talked to anybody from Paradise, only heard stories about them. The group had settled homesteads southeast of Last Stand about ten years prior. They had grouped all their parcels together and had also bought additional acreage over the years. They controlled several thousand acres that they ranched and farmed as a commune. This was the first that he had heard of old Pastor Gordon's death. The pastor had claimed no affiliation with any church, only that he was a direct servant of God and the leader of Paradise. The members only came to Last Stand for necessities and made a point not to socialize with anyone in the town. Paradise even had its own school. There had never been trouble with the group before now. They left the town alone and the town let them be.

"Are you sure that you're sixteen?" Gideon asked.

"I reckon I know how old I am. Yes, I turned sixteen this past May," Charlotte answered.

"And you were going to be forced into a marriage against your wishes?" Gideon questioned.

"I already told you that. Why are you making me repeat all this?" Charlotte asked.

"I'm just double checking to make sure that I have all the facts before somebody shows up looking for you. If you want my help, you might want to start thinking about being a little more polite," Gideon said.

"Yes, sir," Charlotte replied.

"Do you have any family elsewhere where you can go live?" Gideon asked.

"I don't know. We came from Toledo Ohio, but we weren't allowed to stay in touch with our families. Pa has some brothers there. Old Pastor Gordon said that Paradise was all of the family we needed now," she said.

"Of course, he did," Gideon commented.

Finnie walked to the stove and poured more coffee. "What are we going to do with her?" he asked.

"I don't know. It's a ticklish situation. No laws have been broken. We could just send her on her way and let her fend for herself. Get me a cup while you're at it," Gideon said.

"True. I can't imagine that Cecil Hobbs is too thrilled about the arrangement either. Surely they won't marry them if they both oppose the situation," Finnie said as he poured Gideon a cup of coffee.

Charlotte stood up and threw her arms out for emphasis. "Cecil Hobbs is beside himself with excitement. This is the only way anybody would marry him. You have to protect me," she cried out.

"We'd have to keep her in town so that one of us would be around to keep an eye on her. Maybe I can talk Mary into putting her in the spare bedroom in the saloon. Charlotte could clean for her keep until we figure out if she's got family," Gideon said.

Spinning towards Gideon, Charlotte said, "I will not stay in a saloon and consort with that whore. You can forget that."

Gideon jumped to his feet and shook his finger in the girl's face. "Unless you have money for the hotel, you'll stay where I find you a place. You'll be out in the street if I ever hear you call Mary a whore again. Don't judge somebody that you don't even know. Isn't that what your Bible tells you? Now it's my way or get out of here. Which is it?" he yelled.

The girl seemed taken aback by Gideon's outburst and looked down at her feet. "Yes, sir, it won't happen again. I do need your help."

"Is Mary up?" Gideon asked Finnie.

"Could I have a word with you outside?" Finnie requested.

Looking still annoyed, Gideon followed him outside where Finnie caught him up on what had transpired with Mary and his new sleeping arrangement.

"My God, Finnie, I don't know what I'm going to do with you. All you had to do was be excited about the baby and ask her to marry you. It's what you wanted and yet you still messed it up," Gideon said.

"I know. I know. It's just that I was so shocked about the baby that my words came out wrong. I was at a loss at what to say," Finnie said.

"Well, that's a first and a poor time for it to happen. I guess I'm not only the sheriff, but your caretaker too," Gideon said.

"I must confess that I'm about as useful to a woman as a chastity belt in a whorehouse," Finnie said.

Gideon gave Finnie a look and waved his hand through the air. "I'm not even sure what that means," he said as he walked away towards the saloon.

The alley door to the Last Chance was unlocked and Gideon entered to find Mary up and eating breakfast.

"I didn't think that maybe you'd be up so early," Gideon said.

"I wake up early since I threw out that Irish lunkhead," Mary stated.

"I just heard about that. Mary, you're being too hard on Finnie. You surprised him and he chose his words poorly. There are a lot worse things in life, and you know it, and you've seen it. You need to talk to him," Gideon said as he sat down beside her.

"I can't believe that you'd take his side over mine with all that we've been through," Mary said.

"I'm not taking his side so much as I'm trying to help both of you. I'm pretty sure that you both want the same thing, but you've got to give him a chance to make it right. Finnie can be quite the charmer or he can be the yammering fool. You knew that when you took up with him. Look past the flaws to what matters," Gideon said.

"So are you saying that I'm an irrational female?" Mary asked.

"Don't you tell on me, but you're the most rational female that I know, but not this time," Gideon said.

"Okay, enough on this. I'll talk to him, but he better choose his words carefully or I'll choose his grave," Mary said.

Gideon then explained the situation with Charlotte and asked her help.

"Do you really think this is a good idea?" Mary asked.

"No, but it's the only one I have. Finnie or I can keep an eye on things this way. The jail's no place for her. I should warn you that Miss Bell would not win any prizes for sweetness," Gideon said.

"Oh, great. Remind me again why I'm friends with you," Mary said.

Gideon leaned over and kissed her cheek. "I'm too damn charming for my own good," he said before leaving.

Just before noon, four men rode into town. Two of the men rode mules and all looked ragtag except for the one dressed all in black. He appeared short in stature and heavy boned with a taciturn scowl that looked as if it were permanently etched onto his face. Gideon and Finnie waited in front of the jail with shotguns across their laps as the men stopped in front of them.

"Sheriff, I'm Pastor Milton Gordon. One of the members of Paradise has gone missing. We have reason to believe she may have shown up here."

"She has," Gideon replied tersely.

"If you would be so kind as to hand her over to us, we will see that she is taken care of properly. She is young and misguided," Gordon said.

"I'm afraid that I can't do that. She's old enough to decide where she wants to live and who she wants to marry and it isn't Paradise or Cecil Hobbs," Gideon said.

One of the men climbed down from his mule. "See here, Sheriff, that's my daughter and I want to take her home. You have no right to hide her," he said as he loomed over the sitting Gideon.

"Mr. Bell, I suggest that you take a step back or I will do it for you," Gideon said and waited until the man retreated a step. "Your daughter is a legal adult and I can't give her to you. I understand your concerns, but she doesn't want to be part of an arranged marriage. You'll have to respect her wishes."

The pastor straightened his posture in the saddle. "A man like yourself may take marriage lightly, but at Paradise, we try to protect our young ones from the sins of the flesh. We guide them to a suitable partner for life so that they don't make the same mistake as that twofer wife of yours did when she ran off and left her husband for the likes of you. God have mercy on this town with a sheriff that stole another man's wife and a deputy living with a whore."

Anticipating what would next happen, Finnie jumped up and bear hugged Gideon as the sheriff sprung from his seat like a beaver trap snapping. The deputy held firm to prevent Gideon from getting to the pastor and beating the man senseless.

"Gideon, let it go. You're giving him what he wants. Let it go," Finnie pleaded as he easily detained Gideon even as the sheriff's arms flailed away at him.

Gideon continued struggling, and yelled, "Any man I've ever known that worried about everybody else's bedroom, well, they always had a limp tallywag. Is that your problem, do you have a limp tallywag?"

"Sheriff, you haven't seen the last of us," Gordon said before the men rode away.

After the group disappeared out of sight, Finnie released Gideon and watched him pace back and forth in front of the jail while trying to catch his breath.

Finally coming to a stop, Gideon said, "Thank you, I might have killed that son of a bitch. I knew that this would be trouble from the minute I heard about it. People with a Bible and an agenda are more dangerous than all the stagecoach robbers put together. They'll be back for sure."

"I expect that you're right," Finnie said as he dropped back onto the bench.

"I'm going to get Charlotte out of the cell and take her to meet Mary. This should put a cherry on top of my day," Gideon said as the banker, Mr. Fredrick, walked up to the jail.

"Sheriff, your reward money came in today," Mr. Fredrick said.

"Finally, some good news. Mr. Fredrick, I want you to split the money four ways. Put a share in my account and a share in Ethan Oakes' account and then open accounts for Finnegan Ford and Zack Barlow. Finnie can go with you now to sign whatever is necessary and I'll send Zack when I see him," Gideon said.

"As you wish, Sheriff," the banker said.

"Finnie, I suggest that you take a little of your new found wealth and go to the general store and buy a ring. Make Hiram give you a discount. When I'm done with Mary, it's your turn. If you make a mess of things this time, Mary or me is going to shoot you dead," Gideon said.

"Everybody mistreats the Irish. I believe you all think that we're nothing more than a spud with arms and legs," Finnie said as he walked away with Mr. Fredrick.

Gideon retrieved Charlotte from the jail and as they walked to the saloon, he filled her in on what had transpired and warned her about the behavior he expected out of her. They entered the saloon through the alley and Gideon left her in the back room to go find Mary.

Returning with the saloon owner, Gideon said, "Charlotte, this is Mary."

"Glad to meet you," Charlotte said and attempted a curtsy.

"You too. You'll have a nice bedroom all to yourself. We'll get you cleaned up and I'll see if I can find some clothes that fit you," Mary replied.

"Thank you, ma'am."

Anxious to leave, Gideon put his hat back on. "Charlotte, I expect you to do what Mary tells you to do. You'll be working for your room and board. I'm going to contact Toledo and see if they can track down some family that you can go live with."

"Thank you, sir. I appreciate your help," Charlotte said demurely.

After Gideon left, Mary pulled out the tub and began heating water. "It looks like you had a long night. You can take a bath and I'll go try to find you something to wear."

"Were you really a whore?" Charlotte asked.

Mary chuckled. "You don't believe in beating around the bush, but yes I was."

"Did you like it?" the girl asked.

"It beat starving to death. Just like you running away - sometimes we do things that we don't really want to do in order to survive," Mary said.

"I guess that's one way to look at it. I sure would hate to lay with all those men though. Most of them are nasty and stink. I'm not too sure about the whole idea with one that I like and smells good," Charlotte said.

"I wouldn't recommend whoring. Find a good one that you like and keep him. The rest will take care of itself," Mary said.

After filling the tub with hot water, Mary locked the doors to the back room on her way out. She walked to the front of the saloon to check on business before going to find clothes for Charlotte. Finnie sat waiting at the bar when she entered.

"May I have a word with you in private?" Finnie asked.

"I have to go upstairs and find some clothes for Charlotte. You can come along," Mary said.

He followed her up the front stairs and into the room that they shared. Finnie quickly closed the door behind them before dropping to one knee and holding up the gold ring he had purchased.

"Mary Sawyer, I can't think of anything on earth that I want more than to help you raise our baby and to spend the rest of my life with you. You make me happier than I've ever been in my life. Will you marry me?" Finnie said.

Mary tried to hold her emotion in check, but in looking down at the earnest expression on the little Irishman, her eyes teared up, and she swiped them away. "Finnegan Ford, you're a lot of trouble, but I do love you. Yes, I will marry you."

Standing up, Finnie placed the ring on her finger. "We do things lively, don't we? Never a dull moment. We'll have to talk to Ethan about marrying us."

"Can you believe that we're really having a baby? I still can't believe it," Mary said and threw her arms around her shorter fiancé.

"I hope this baby gets its height from you," he said.

"Shh – we don't care how tall he or she is. We'll love them short or tall, just like I love your little sawed-off ass," Mary whispered in his ear.

# Chapter 16

Digging a well proved to be a lot of work and not much fun either. Zack began digging a hole with a five foot diameter and so far had managed to go about four feet deep into the ground. After chopping through some roots near the top, digging became easier and no rocks had impeded his progress as he methodically slung the dirt out of the hole. A large pile of soil was already taking shape that would also have to be dealt with before long. The day was unusually hot for September and as he worked, the soil clung to his sweaty clothes and skin until he could pass for some kind of dirt-man.

He and Joann chose a spot for the cabin near a grove of cottonwoods. The land sloped gently towards a creek and would make for a good yard and place to build a barn later. Their home would sit about fifty yards from the creek that ran good water year round. Zack kept reminding himself that Gideon and Ethan had both assured him that water tables were highest near cottonwood patches. He already felt as if he were digging to China.

Joann had decided to make the trip with him that day. She fluttered around like a bird as he worked, talking nonstop as he dug the hole. In her mind's eye, she could see the cabin and barn already completed. She chattered about the layout of their home and what they could purchase for it with the reward money. Zack listened part of the time and ignored her when concentrating on the work at hand.

Stopping in front of Zack, Joann asked, "What are we going to do with all of that dirt?"

"We need to borrow Ethan's wagon. I figure that you can sling the dirt into it while I dig and then you can haul it away. It'll be good for you – put a little muscle on those bones," Zack said.

"I helped Papa do lots of hard work. I can do that, but I never heard you complain about my bones before," she said.

"I'm not complaining, but you are kind of scrawny. You might blow away out here," Zack teased.

"I'll make you think scrawny the next time that you want a good look at my scrawny ass," Joann shot back.

Grinning at his wife, Zack said, "You couldn't stand to live without it now."

"So you say. I'm so excited about living here. Just think, we are going to build our place just like our ancestors did that settled this land. We won't have the Indians to fight, but we'll have plenty of other challenges. We can raise our babies here and grow old sitting out on our porch. Take a break and let's go for a walk," Joann said.

"I can't. You'll be complaining later that the hole doesn't look any deeper. We aren't ever going to make those dreams come true unless I get things done and there's a whole lot of things need doing before you even begin mentioning babies," he said.

"You're no fun. If you don't want to bake bread, you shouldn't play with the oven so much," Joann said and flittered away.

Zack resumed shoveling out the well, concentrating on one scoop at a time, and didn't realize Joann was gone until he noticed how quiet things had become. Looking around, he didn't see her anywhere.

"Joann, are you okay?" he called out.

"Zack, did you know that this creek has a pool. My scrawny ass is floating in it buck naked for all the world to see. I guess you're probably too busy to come see for yourself. It's mighty cold. Do you have any ideas on how I could get warm?" Joann yelled.

Grinning, Zack climbed out of the hole. He decided that he might be too busy digging a well to take a walk, but some things in life could not wait.

∞

John still required a lot of rest. He spent a large portion of each day sleeping in Doc's back room while the doctor tended to patients. After treating his last patient for the day, Doc walked to the door of the back room and could hear his son snoring. The doctor decided to use the opportunity to get out of the office for a while and put his hat on to walk to the Last Chance.

Mary stood behind the bar when he entered the saloon. Sitting down at his usual table, she brought him a beer without his asking and sat down with him.

"You're looking pretty today. I believe that carrying that baby agrees with you," Doc said.

"Thank you, Doc. I do feel good," Mary said.

"I heard about Gideon sticking you with that girl. How's that working?" the doctor asked.

"Pretty good, actually. She's a good worker. Gideon warned me about her, but I think he must have laid the law down because she hasn't given me any trouble. She

LAST RIDE • 111

sure is curious about the whore trade though," she said and laughed.

The doctor chuckled. "I would imagine after a life lived at Paradise that her image of this place must have been like Sodom and Gomorrah. The saloon probably hasn't lived up to her imagination," Doc said and took a sip of beer.

"Let's hope not. How is John?" Mary asked.

"He's getting stronger every day, but still sleeps a lot. I think the whole thing is awkward for both of us. We've been thrown together a little too much by circumstance while he recovers. I don't know quite how to act and I don't think that he does either," Doc said.

"That's to be expected. I think you should treat him like a new friend and not think about him being your son. Who would have ever thought that you and Finnie would hit it off? Approach him like that. At his age, it's not as if he's a child needing a father. You may find you have a lot in common or you may not, but I'm sure that you'll get along. And deep down, no matter what, you'll both know that you have a bond. Just let it take a natural course," Mary said.

"That's a good idea. I knew I came over here to see you for a reason. Working in a saloon must give you insight into every sort of human nature," Doc said.

Mary laughed. "Some that I'd just as soon not know."

"I'll give it a try," Doc said.

"Take him in your buggy to see the mountains and stop in to visit Ethan and Sarah and run by Abby's place. You'll get yourself into trouble with those two ladies if you don't introduce him anyway," Mary suggested.

"You're full of good ideas. Oh, by the way, I hear that congratulations are in order. Finnie came over to the office and told me. His chest was sticking out so far that I thought that he was going to bust his buttons," the doctor said.

Mary held out her hand to show off her gold band. "See my ring. I do love that little Irishman. He about drives me crazy, but I love him. I know that we make an odd pair, but it works at least most of the time," she said with a smile.

"Look at the bright side. There'll never be a dull moment with Finnegan Ford as your husband. You'll either be laughing or cussing at him all the time," Doc said.

"That you can count on," Mary chimed in.

"And I think that he'll make a fine father for that baby too," he said.

"I know he will. God knows what that poor little baby is going to look like," Mary said as the two of them laughed.

# Chapter 17

Walking out of the jail, Gideon spied Ethan on his wagon headed his way. The wagon pulled to a stop in front of the building.

"You look hard at it," Gideon said.

"Nah, I had to come to town for some feed for the horses," Ethan said as he climbed off the wagon.

"I haven't had a chance to tell you, but the reward money came in and I had it put into your account," Gideon said.

"I had to stop in the bank and Mr. Fredrick told me. Much obliged," Ethan said.

"What are you going to do with all your new found wealth?" Gideon asked.

"Sarah decided that the cabin is big enough. It won't be that many years until Benjamin moves on and the two of us don't need the extra space. I'm a bit relieved to tell you the truth. I stopped by the general store and had Hiram order a set of china and a pearl ring for Sarah. I'm going to surprise her with them. She's done without long enough. It's the least I can do," Ethan said.

"Well, aren't you the romantic? I ordered Abby a gold picture locket. It's going to have her initials engraved on the front and Hiram took a picture of all three of the kids to put in it. I can't wait to get it, the engraving seems to be slowing down its arrival," Gideon said.

"Well, we should make both of our wives happy," Ethan remarked as he followed Gideon into the jail.

"Tell Zack about the money. I probably won't see them until Sunday," Gideon said as he took his seat.

"I will. That boy has begun digging his well. He's about tuckered out," Ethan said and sat down in a chair.

"I didn't know that he was going to start without me or you helping him. I hope he knows what he's doing. I don't need Joann becoming a widow," Gideon said.

"He says he's helped dig a couple of them in Wyoming. I went to check it and the soil looks firm. I think he'll be fine and I figured that maybe this Sunday the two of us could go help him," Ethan said.

"I should've never brought that boy to Last Stand. I didn't realize all the trouble he'd cause me," Gideon joked.

"You don't mean that. He makes a pretty good son-in-law," Ethan said.

"You're right, but it gives me something to complain about. I'm practicing to be like Doc when I get old. Sometimes it does feel as if I gained another person to have to watch over," Gideon said.

"I suppose that's true, but he has come in handy a time or two. We wouldn't know what to do without him now," Ethan said.

"Since you're a preacher, what do you know about Paradise?" Gideon inquired.

"Not much. They're not exactly friendly towards the other churches. In fact, they've always been downright hostile," Ethan said.

"I kind of figured that. The old man died and now his son is running things. I got a girl that ran away from there because they were going to force her to marry," Gideon said.

"I don't know what to tell you besides they have a low opinion of all the rest of us," Ethan said.

"You're not telling me anything that I don't know," Gideon said.

"Well, I have to get home. Just wanted to stop by and say hi," Ethan said as he arose from his seat.

"I'll walk you out. I need to find Finnie anyway," Gideon said.

Gideon walked down the street until he found Finnie talking to Mayor Hiram Howard in front of his general store.

"Is he trying to get my job?" Gideon asked the mayor.

"No, he's just telling stories on you," Hiram said.

"I don't doubt it. Talking is his strong suit," Gideon said.

"I've got customers to tend to. Did you need me?" Hiram asked.

"No, I was tracking down my deputy. Good to see you, Hiram," Gideon said.

After the mayor returned inside his store, Finnie said, "What's up?"

"We're going to take a little ride to Paradise," Gideon said.

"You're not going to let go of what he said about Abby and Mary, are you?" Finnie asked.

"Probably not," Gideon replied.

The wind had shifted to out of the west and cooled things back down to a normal temperature. Gideon wore Jack's coat to ward off the chill even though the sky was clear and sunny. The land southwest of Last Stand flattened out into a hint of the plains farther to the east and made for easy travel. Finnie, in a fine mood from his impending marriage, sang Irish tunes as they rode until Gideon started a meaningless conversation just to shut him up.

For the most part, the inhabitants of Paradise lived on their homesteads, but a mini-village had sprung up around the church that included a hall, blacksmith shop, furniture maker, and four houses. All looked in good condition with fresh coats of paint that made for a tranquil appearance. The number of people walking around the village surprised Gideon as he rode up. The crowd quickly scurried to the church upon seeing the riders. Pastor Gordon appeared on the steps of the church by the time Gideon and Finnie pulled their horses to a stop.

"Sheriff, this is private property. You need a warrant to be here," Pastor Gordon said before they had time to dismount.

"I'm not searching for anything. I'm just paying a friendly visit," Gideon said as the church members gathered around their pastor.

With contempt dripping in his voice, Gordon said, "I'm not surprised that you wear a jacket made by those pagan Indians. It would go in keeping with your heathen ways."

"I see that you are not much for Mark 12:31. Love thy neighbor doesn't seem to be high on your list," Gideon said with a snicker.

"Where is Charlotte?" the pastor demanded.

"Oh, she's in good hands. Mary is taking care of her at the saloon," Gideon answered.

"Damn your soul to hell. How dare you take one of God's children and cast her lot with prostitutes. 'Do not prostitute thy daughter, to cause her to be a whore; lest the land fall to whoredom, and the land become full of wickedness.' Sheriff Johann, you are that wickedness. You are an evil man and will know the bowels of hell," Gordon shouted in his sermon voice.

Looking at the crowd standing around the pastor, Gideon said, "Any of you that don't want to be forced into a marriage, come see me in town. We'll provide for you. Spread the word."

"Get off this land. If you think that you are going to persecute this church, you have another thing coming. As the Lord's shepherd, I will see you smitten down like a wolf trying to attack the flock," Gordon screamed.

Looking at Finnie, Gideon said, "Did that sound like a threat to you, Finnie?"

"I believe it did," Finnie answered.

"Pastor, since I'm in a fine mood, I'm going to let your threat slide this time, but I'll be waiting for you if you ever want to make good on it, but you better bring something more powerful than your hateful hot air. Have a blessed day," Gideon said and spun Buck around, riding away at a leisurely pace.

"What did all that accomplish?" Finnie asked as he caught up with the sheriff.

"I came to let those people know that they didn't have to have an arranged marriage if they didn't want one. The rest of it was just icing on the cake," Gideon said.

"He really got on your bad side, didn't he?" Finnie remarked.

"He should've never brought Abby and Mary into this. He can say what he wants about me, but I will make him regret talking about them," Gideon said, contempt rising in his voice with each word.

"What do you think he will do?" Finnie asked.

"I don't have a clue.  Probably nothing," Gideon said and kneed Buck into a lope.

# Chapter 18

Lunchtime filled the Last Chance with customers ranging from cowboys to store owners. Ever since Mary began offering the free meal with a drink purchase, business had exploded much to the chagrin of the hotel's restaurant. One drink usually led to two and profit for the saloon owner. Gideon and Finnie sat at their usual table watching Mary and Charlotte darting around to keep up with demand.

As Charlotte brought the two lawmen their food, Gideon said, "I heard back from the sheriff in Toledo and he hasn't located your family yet, but he's still checking into it."

"Thank you, Sheriff. God hasn't smitten me down yet for working in a saloon and I'm pretty good at it or at least Mary tells me that I am," Charlotte said.

"I think you are. Maybe God isn't as harsh as some would lead us to believe," Gideon said.

"No, sir, maybe not. I have to get back to work," she said before scurrying away.

Finnie took a drink of his beer. "She's sure a lot friendlier than our first meeting," he said as he set down his beer.

"That she is. Changing the subject, Mary's not going to be able to run around like that much longer. It'll be too hard on her," Gideon said.

"I know it. We've been talking about things and trying to figure out everything," Finnie said.

Grinning at his friend, Gideon said, "Your life is about to get a lot more complicated."

Ignoring the observation, Finnie asked, "What are we going to do about the hangings?"

"Unless something new comes up, there's not much that we can do. You can't arrest somebody if you don't have a suspect," Gideon said.

"You really don't think his neighbor did it?" Finnie asked between bites of food.

"Not really and we couldn't prove it if he did. We're pretty sure that there was more than one. Maybe somebody will get loose-lipped," Gideon said.

Finnie nodded his head before asking, "You've taken a shine to that jacket, haven't you?"

"I guess it's my way of keeping Jack's memory alive. I do feel responsible for his death. I should've known he was too old to ask him to ride with me. We weren't going on a picnic, but chasing a murderer," Gideon said.

"He seemed fit enough when I met him last year," Finnie remarked.

"Oh, he was fit enough, but he got careless. We've all done it, but I think he'd beat death so many times that he thought that he could charm bullets to miss him," Gideon said.

"Don't be so hard on yourself. Nothing good will come from it. If there ever was a more independent cuss that did as he pleased, I've never come across him," Finnie said.

By the time they finished their meals, the lunch crowd had thinned out, and Mary joined them at the table. "Has Finnie told you about our plans?" she asked.

"Not exactly," Gideon answered.

Mary gave her husband-to-be a look of dismay before speaking. "We're going to try to find a house in town. I'm going to keep the baby here with me during the

LAST RIDE • 121

days until it's old enough to be watched at home and Delta will quit the trade to run things in the evening. I didn't want the whoring going on any longer anyway. We'll be home every night with the baby."

"You're going to need more help. You aren't going to be able to run around at lunch like you did today much longer and I'm not sure you can work with a baby here either. At least if that baby is anything like Chance," Gideon said.

"You're no fun. We'll hire somebody to watch the baby here, but I'll have to take breaks to feed it," Mary chided.

"You're going to spend all of poor Finnie's reward money," Gideon teased.

"Poor Finnie is the reason I'm this way," Mary said with a giggle. "We'll be fine, especially if nobody ever reopens the Lucky Horse."

"Maybe you should buy the Lucky Horse just to make sure it stays closed and you could always open it back up if you want to be a saloon tycoon," Gideon said.

Finnie cleared his throat. "You two are rattling like a church bell. It's a sad day when an Irishman can't get a word in edgewise. I feel like the roasted pig on the table with an apple shoved in my mouth."

"You're right about your life being cooked for sure. You'll be washing out diapers and singing Irish lullabies here shortly," Gideon teased.

Charlotte walked up to the table and stood beside Mary.

"If you don't mind, I'm going to go to the store and buy a bow with the money you gave me," Charlotte said.

"I didn't give it to you. You earned it. I'll see you later," Mary said.

"That seems to be working out well," Gideon said as Charlotte walked out of the saloon.

"Yes, it is. I'd love to hire her if she ends up staying in Last Stand," Mary said.

"Finnie, we better get out of here. The townsfolk will be thinking that they're not getting their money's worth out of us," Gideon said.

Gideon left for a meeting with the mayor and the city council. Even though he had now been elected to the position of sheriff, they still liked to meet with him regularly as if he remained their appointee. For the most part, Gideon played along to keep from ruffling feathers and only pushed back when necessary.

Some of the council members were not thrilled with Charlotte working in the Last Chance for fear of upsetting the Paradise congregation and causing its members to back their own candidate. Gideon defended his decision to protect the girl and then asked the council if any of them would like to volunteer to keep her. The council quickly moved on to another topic at that point.

With the meeting finally adjourned, Gideon walked back to the jail to find Finnie and Mary waiting for him there.

Looking at the expressions on their faces, Gideon said, "This can't be good. What is it?"

"Charlotte never came back to the saloon. Finnie and I went all around town and nobody saw her after she bought her bow," Mary said.

"Damn it. How in the hell did they take her in broad daylight and nobody see a thing. They're more brazen than I thought. Well, there's nothing left to do, but go out there and get her," Gideon said.

After Mary headed back to the saloon, Finnie said, "You know that they're not going to give her up without a fight."

"I know, but they don't have the guts to shoot us. I bet that if I'd knock the shit out of Gordon, the rest would hightail it like scalded dogs. Let's quit talking and start riding," Gideon said as he checked his rifle.

About halfway to Paradise, Finnie spotted a hair bow lying off to the side of the road. Stopping, he climbed down and picked it up. "I guess this ends any doubt," he said before stuffing the item into his saddlebag.

Nobody lingered outside in the little village as they rode into the churchyard, but Gideon spied five men in open windows in the various buildings. No rifles were in view, but he realized that the men were surely armed. "I may have misjudged their will to fight," he said to Finnie.

Pastor Gordon and Charlotte walked out of the church and into the yard. The girl had tears running down her cheeks and stared down at her feet, refusing to make eye contact with Gideon. Her pitiful state made her appear younger than her sixteen years.

"Sheriff Johann, we've been expecting you," Gordon said.

"I see that you have," Gideon said as he purposely glanced at the men in the windows.

"Charlotte has something to say to you, Sheriff," Gordon said.

The girl hesitated in speaking and the pastor started tapping his foot in agitation.

Finally looking up, Charlotte said, "Sheriff, I'm sorry for any inconvenience I've caused you, but I wanted to go home where I belong. I've decided to marry Cecil."

The pastor took a step towards Gideon's horse. "See, Sheriff, you stuck your nose where it didn't belong. 'And they may come to their senses and escaped from the snare of the devil, having been held captive by him to do his will.' You can leave now."

Finnie reached into his saddlebag and pulled out the bow. "You lost your bow," he said and held it out to Charlotte.

"You must be mistaken, Mr. Finnie. It is shameful to wear one's hair with adornment," Charlotte said.

Gideon climbed down from his horse and stepped towards the girl. He could see the sunlight reflecting off the rifles of the men in the windows now. Charlotte looked so miserable that his paternal instincts kicked in so that he wanted to hug her and tell her that everything would be all right. "Charlotte, you do not have to stay here. I'm the law and they can't kidnap you like this. I will take you back to Last Stand and do a better job of protecting you this time. I promise," he said, emotion rising in his voice.

"Mr. Gideon, I came back to Paradise of my own freewill. I appreciate your concern, but you can go. I want to stay," Charlotte said.

"What have they threatened you with? Damn it, I'm the law and they can't do this," Gideon yelled.

Charlotte, crying loudly, turned and ran into the church.

"Sheriff, do not swear in my presence. Now get out of here before we are forced to defend ourselves," Gordon spat out.

"Go to hell, you charlatan," Gideon yelled as he climbed onto Buck and rode away.

Finnie didn't catch Gideon until the sheriff had slowed the horse to a walk.

"What are we going to do now?' Finnie asked.

"There's not a damn thing that we can do. They succeeded in putting the fear of God into that girl," Gideon said, anger still in his voice.

"What if we arrested her for something so that we could hold her at the jail?" Finnie suggested.

"That might work until the judge showed up and then all hell would break loose. We'd probably end up locked in our own jail. And besides, I was wrong. I believe they would've killed us today," Gideon said.

"They beat us," Finnie said with resignation.

# Chapter 19

Tears streamed down Mary's face as she sat at a table in the saloon with Finnie, Doc, and Gideon the day after Charlotte's return to Paradise. The crying took Finnie a bit by surprise. Mary usually took adversity with grit and seldom gave in to crying, but Charlotte's blight had upset her terribly.

"Charlotte's arranged marriage is not much different than those poor girls forced into prostitution at the Lucky Horse last year. It might as well be slavery," Mary blubbered out.

"There's nothing that I can do if she says it's what she wants," Gideon said, trying to sound more convincing than he felt.

"You're being a tad bit emotional about it, don't you think?" Finnie said.

"Of course, a man would say that. You've never been in a situation where you have to be with somebody that repulses you. It can make you hate yourself," Mary cried.

"I just meant that usually you get mad and ready to fight instead of crying," Finnie said defensively.

"I know. I don't know what's wrong with me. Usually I'd be ready to grab my shotgun and go to town," Mary said.

"It's the baby. It did the same thing to Abby. She'd cry at the drop of a hat," Gideon said.

"You men think you know everything," Mary remarked.

"He's right, at least this time," Doc said with a smile. "I've doctored enough pregnant women to know that the baby does something to them to make for mood swings. You'll get back to being your mean old self after you give birth."

"Yes, and I might put an end to everybody at this table when I do. You're certainly not a sympathetic lot today," Mary said.

John walked into the Last Chance. He had just gone on a shopping spree and entered the saloon dressed in clothes that could have been borrowed from Gideon's wardrobe, right down to the hat and boots. Only the lack of a gun strapped to his side and his neatly trimmed hair prevented him from passing as Gideon's stockier built double.

Mary looked up and smiled. "Looks like Last Stand has us a new cowboy."

"Don't make fun of me. Doc is taking me for a ride in his buggy and I didn't think a banker's suit would be appropriate clothing. This is much more comfortable," John said in his defense.

"You just need a little sun and windburn to look the part. If I hadn't given up the bottle for Mary, I could teach you the finer points of cowboy drinking," Finnie said.

"I think I'll pass on that. Banker drinking is bad enough," John said.

Doc smiled at his son. "You'll be moving your family out here and going into the cattle business before you know it. I bet your wife would love that."

"She'd probably adjust better than I would. Boston society wears on her sometimes," John said.

Mary turned to Gideon. "Are you sure that there's nothing that you can do for Charlotte?"

"Mary, I don't think they're going to let her out of their sight this time. I can't just go in there and take her. If I had tried yesterday, I believe they would've killed Finnie and me. That bunch is not rational," Gideon said.

Standing up, Doc said, "John and I are going to go for a buggy ride. We best get to it." He and John then departed the saloon and headed for the stable.

After leaving town, Doc's buggy moved smartly down the road as he and John took their first ride together. Much of John's color had returned to his face and he had begun walking the town to regain his strength. His excitement over the excursion was palpable and had spread to the doctor as well. The pair had been near giddy as they climbed into the cart.

"My God, this land is beautiful. No wonder you came out here and stayed," John said as they traveled away farther from the town.

"That it is. Sometimes I take it for granted and then something will catch my eye and I realize that I'm in God's country," the doctor said.

"I would say so. No book or picture can do this panorama justice," John said.

Before them loomed the highest peaks surrounding Last Stand. The mountains stood bare of vegetation, reflecting shades of white and gray in the sunlight. Sheer cliffs dropping hundreds of feet covered the sides and gave the impression that even a mountain goat could not navigate the terrain. Snow coated the highest peaks and hinted at what lie in store for the coming winter. Down below in the tree line, a bull elk grazed, raising its head to sniff the wind and showing off its magnificent antlers.

"Look at that beast.  Have you ever eaten one of them?" John asked.

"Well, not a whole one, but yes I've eaten elk.  It's taste somewhat like beef but has a wild taste to it.  It's quite good," Doc said.

"I need to try that before I head back," John remarked.

"I'll see to it that it happens," Doc promised.

"What was it like when you first moved out here?" John asked.

"As wild as things can get these days, it used to be a lot worse, especially after the war.  A lot of riffraff headed west to make their fortunes.  Sheriff Fuller cleaned things up back then.  An outlaw named Durango Dick showed up at my doorstep with a gunshot wound and waving a revolver in my face.  I tried to get him to put the gun down so that I could treat him, but he would have no part of it so I grabbed my shotgun behind the door and blew him into the street.  Nobody messed with me after that," Doc said.

"You killed a man?" John asked in astonishment.

"I did.  I wasn't about to go probing a wound with a gun pointed at me," Doc said.

"Did it bother you?"

"Not really.  I figured one dead outlaw prevented at least two innocent people from losing their lives," Doc answered.

"Amazing.  I can tell everybody that my father is a doctor and a deadly gunman.  That will catch their attention.  Sounds a lot more interesting than being a banker," John said with a laugh.

With eyes misting over at John's mention of 'my father', Doc turned his head away as if gazing to the west. After all the years of burying the knowledge that he was a father with a son back east somewhere that he had never seen, that illusion was now shattered as suddenly as a teacup dropped to the floor. The juxtaposition seemed almost dizzying. Inhaling a big breath, he steeled his emotion. "It was a long time ago," he said meekly.

"I have to talk Kate and the kids into coming out here. Everybody needs to see country like this," John gushed, oblivious to what had just transpired.

"You think she will?" Doc asked.

"I don't know if I can talk her into spending that much time on a train with a toddler. That would be a challenge," John said with a laugh.

"I sure would like that," Doc remarked.

"You need to come to Boston too. Is there a photography studio in Last Stand? We should have our portrait made together," John said.

"Hiram Howard has a back room in his general store where he makes portraits. Most of the families around here have their picture made there," Doc said.

"We need to do it then," John said.

The two men arrived at Gideon's cabin in the early afternoon. Abby answered the door with Chance in her arms, surprised by the arrival of company.

"Doc, I wasn't expecting you," Abby said.

"Abby, I would like you to meet John," Doc said and hesitated before adding, "This is my son."

Extending her hand, Abby said, "Good to meet you. I wondered when I would get the opportunity."

John held out his arms to Chance. The toddler smiled and willingly came to him. "Nobody would have to tell me that this is Gideon's son. He looks just like him. I miss my little one terribly."

"Do you think so? Sometimes I'm not so sure," Abby said as she led the two men into the cabin.

"I would bet he's the spitting image of Gideon at this age. Doc should remember," John said.

"Do you know how many babies I've doctored in my lifetime? Too many to remember what they all looked like. I believe you are correct, but I can't say for sure. I do remember Gideon's blue eyes and Chance certainly has those," Doc said.

Abby made coffee and dished out pieces of apple pie as the three of them talked. John told Abby all about his family and Boston while she talked about her life in Last Stand and her daughters, Joann and Winnie. Doc barely spoke as John and Abby carried on as if they had known each other all their lives.

Interrupting the conversation, Doc said, "We need to get going. We still have to see Ethan and Sarah."

"Doc, you old dog. You came here first so that you could wrangle a meal out of Sarah," Abby said.

"Abby, you are a fine cook. You know I adore it," Doc said.

"I wasn't talking about my cooking and you avoided commenting on what I said," Abby said with a smile.

Doc grinned mischievously. "I'm not in the habit of comparing women's cooking. I'm much too old and wise for that. I will say that that apple pie you served might have been the finest I've ever eaten though."

"I'll serve you boiled shoe leather the next time you show up," Abby said.

John hold out his hand to Abby, "Abby, it has been my pleasure to meet you. You are a lovely person. If I would have been in Gideon's place, I assure you that I wouldn't have waited eighteen years to return."

"Get out of here, you two. Flattery will only get you so far. You are much sweeter than your father," Abby said and stuck her tongue out at Doc.

The two men waved goodbye and headed towards Ethan's place. Ethan sat on his porch blowing plumes of smoke from his pipe as the buggy pulled into the yard. Zack sat beside him scratching the ear of the family dog. The two men had finished culling cattle a little earlier than Ethan had expected and had called it a day. Upon seeing the buggy, Ethan stood and hollered for Sarah to come join them.

"Did you give up doctoring and take up the carriage service business?" Ethan hollered out.

"No, John needed to see some mountains," Doc said as Sarah walked out onto the porch.

"Hello, Doc," she called out.

"Sarah and Zack, I want you to meet John," Doc said.

With the greetings out of the way, Doc looked at the three men standing before him and said to John, "Can you guess what you have in common with these two?"

John looked the two over before saying, "I can't say that I can. I would guess that they are capable of doing a whole host of things that I would be ill-equipped to perform."

"I've treated all three of you for gunshot wounds. If Gideon were here, it would make four," Doc said.

"Really?" John said in amazement. "That's incredible. This really is a wild country. And which one of us came closest to dying?"

"That would be Ethan. A lesser man would've never survived. He had me scared. Gideon came in a close second. His was from lack of treatment. If Benjamin hadn't found him, he would have ended up a pile of bones that the wolves dragged off," Doc said.

"The good Lord needed me to keep educating Ethan before he sent him on to Heaven. I made him into the man that he is today," Sarah said to a round of laughter.

"John wants to try elk. Do you have any?" the doctor asked.

"No, we've eaten all that we have. Sarah and I were just talking about me needing to go shoot us one," Ethan said.

"I got a great idea. This Sunday after church we will invite Gideon's family, Zack and Joann, Finnie and Mary, and you two over for an elk feast," Sarah said.

"That's providing that I can get an elk between now and then," Ethan said.

"You're always bragging about your hunting prowess and how you're a better shot than Gideon. I can't imagine that you'll let us down," Sarah said to seal the deal.

Ethan grinned at his wife. "This is the thanks I get for being kind enough to give you a son."

Sarah let out a laugh. "I'm sure that the men here believe that about as much as I do. I don't think giving me a son was what you were worried about accomplishing."

"Okay, you two. John might not be used to such conversation from where he comes from," Doc said.

Sarah laughed again. "I bet he is if he's your son. Why don't you stay for supper? Benjamin will be home soon and John can meet him."

"Sarah, you know I never turn down your cooking. That's the only reason I came out here when you were nursing Gideon back to health. It probably saved his life," Doc said.

# Chapter 20

Ominous clouds had rolled into Last Stand the previous day. The skies looked so dark and threatening that the mood of the town turned somber and slowed business at the Last Chance. By evening, the rains started and sometime after midnight turned to snow. Gideon traipsed through six inches of the white powder with ice beneath it to get to town the next morning. He threw extra wood into the stove and lit a roaring fire, knocking the chill out of the air by the time that Finnie trudged in, stomping the snow off his boots in the doorway.

"It's a sad day when I can ride all the way from the cabin in this weather and have this place warmed before you show up from down the street," Gideon said irritably.

"I'm afraid it is true, but I couldn't bring myself to climb out of the covers this morning. Mary and our bed felt a whole a lot warmer than this jail. You know how I hate snow and cold," Finnie said.

"Well, you picked the wrong place to live then. Maybe you should move to Texas," Gideon snapped back.

"And it makes you grouchy," Finnie said.

"Do you want some coffee or not?" Gideon said as a peace offering.

"I'd love some. With a little sugar, please," Finnie said with a smile.

An hour later, Paul Sellers walked into the jail, his face red from the cold and his beard icy from his breath.

He was an area rancher with a big enough spread to have a couple of full-time ranch hands. Known as a taciturn man with little sense of humor, he nonetheless remained well respected in the community.

"Paul, what brings you to town on such a miserable day?" Gideon asked as the rancher clapped his hands to aid circulation.

"Bad news, Sheriff. My ranch hand, Theo Sullenger, didn't show up today so I went looking for him. I found him and his woman hanged. They look to have been there all night. I had let them build a little cabin on my place. They were good people," Paul said.

A chill washed over Gideon and he shuddered. His gnawing fear that the hangings of Roy and Sissy would not be an isolated incident had just been confirmed. He felt powerless to get out of his chair and looked at Paul blankly before collecting himself.

"Is their cabin within view of your place?" Gideon asked.

"No, it's a good half-mile away over some hills," Paul answered.

"Did you see anything unusual yesterday?" Gideon inquired.

"No, but I certainly didn't spend any time outdoors last night," Paul said.

"We'll ride back with you and you can show us where they are," Gideon said in resignation.

"I'll go get my horse," Finnie said as he put on his coat.

The three men made a solemn ride back to the ranch. The scene looked much the same as the previous hangings. Both bodies had their hands bound behind their backs and looked to have put up a gallant struggle before their death. Their bodies showed signs of bruising and had busted lips and bloody noses. One of Theo's arms bent down at an unnatural angle. The only tracks in the snow were from Paul having discovered the bodies earlier in the day.

After cutting the bodies down from the tree, "Gideon asked, "Do you know of anybody that Theo had problems with?"

"No, Theo wasn't like most ranch hands. He and Wanda were homebodies. I let him build the cabin to make sure that he didn't leave me. He's the best ranch hand I ever had. It's a shame – never caused anybody any problems. I guess I'll bury them in our family plot if Theo's brother doesn't object. I don't think Wanda has family in these here parts," Paul said.

Inside the cabin there were obvious signs of a struggle. Two chairs were turned over and a cup lay shattered on the floor. Finnie found a few drops of blood.

"The murderers got bolder this time," Gideon said.

"Yeah, it looks like they forced their way in," Finnie said.

"Sheriff, why do you think this happened?" Paul asked.

"I don't know. I'll go talk to Wendell to let him know and see if he has any ideas. Do you need help with the bodies?" Gideon said.

"No, I'll go get the buckboard and my other men can help me load them. I'll start making boxes and you can send word on what Wendell wants," Paul said.

"I'll do it," Gideon said before he and Finnie rode away.

After they had covered some ground, Finnie asked, "And what do you make of all this? There seems to be no rhyme or reason to either of these hangings."

"I know it, but there surely is. Maybe Wendell can shed some light," Gideon replied.

Wendell Sullenger worked in the feed store. He was a short man bulked up with muscle from years of hoisting sacks of feed. Gideon found him standing behind the counter when he entered the building.

"What can I do for you, Sheriff?" Wendell asked.

"Wendell, I have some bad news. Theo and Wanda have been murdered out on Paul Sellers' ranch," Gideon said.

Dropping with a thud into a chair, Wendell asked, "Who would do such a thing, Sheriff?"

"I don't know, Wendell. I was hoping that maybe you could help me figure that out," Gideon said.

"Theo didn't have many friends, but he didn't have any enemies. He wasn't that kind of a man," Wendell said.

"I didn't think so. Were Theo and Wanda married, by chance?" Gideon asked.

"Nah, they always talked about making it legal but they never did. Theo wasn't much for that kind of thing," Wendell said.

"Paul is willing to bury them on his family plot if you don't object," Gideon said.

"That'd be fine. I'll ride out there to pay my respects and let him know," Wendell said.

Gideon watched Wendell's expression. The man looked too shocked to even begin to grieve and Gideon wished he knew a way to comfort him. He couldn't even think of anything else to say. Finally, he walked behind the counter and patted Wendell's shoulder.

"I'll be fine, Sheriff. It's just a little hard to take in right now. You go catch the murderer," Wendell said.

"I'll do my best," Gideon said before he and Finnie walked back to the jail.

After throwing some wood into the stove, Finnie asked, "What are you thinking?"

"I think that it's no coincidence that both hangings happened before bad weather and I don't think it's a coincidence that both couples weren't married," Gideon said.

"And considering that we found a cross and already know that there's trouble in Paradise, pardon the pun, I'd say we have some suspects," Finnie said.

"Let's go take a ride after we warm up," Gideon said.

"In this cold weather? You're going to freeze my Irish manhood right off. Irish men make for poor eunuchs. We like our pleasures," Finnie said.

"I always thought that you made for a poor everything. Don't worry, I'll see to it that it gets a proper burial," Gideon said.

"That'll be a mighty big hole that you'll have to dig," Finnie said.

Gideon and Finnie rode into Paradise. The only signs of life were plumes of smoke escaping the chimneys. Climbing down from his horse, Gideon walked briskly into the church before anyone could discover them and come to meet them outdoors. Finnie remained sitting on his horse. Pastor Gordon, Cecil's father, and three other men sat around a potbelly stove. Their conversation stopped abruptly upon seeing the sheriff.

"Sheriff Johann, have you come to be saved?" Gordon asked.

"Not today. I was in the neighborhood and thought I'd check to see if Charlotte had a change of mind," Gideon said.

"Charlotte is now Mrs. Cecil Hobbs. She is enjoying the bliss of a holy matrimony and no longer will be tempted by the lust of the devil and his treachery. The newlyweds are in their own home," the pastor said.

"That girl's now my daughter-in-law. Don't you worry about her. She's in a fine family now," the elder Hobbs said.

"She didn't seem too interested in marriage or being a Hobbs either. I think you all are the ones with the temptation problems," Gideon said as he scanned the hands of the men. None of them showed any signs of cuts or bruises on their knuckles from what he could see, but Mr. Hobbs clearly had a busted lip.

"You can leave now, Sheriff. Unless you plan to make an arrest you can get out of here," Gordon said.

"Mr. Hobbs, did Charlotte punch you in the mouth when you tried to welcome her into the family?" Gideon asked.

"Don't you worry about my lip. I slipped on the ice," Mr. Hobbs said.

"Leave, Sheriff. I know the law," Gordon said, his voice rising just short of a yell.

"Good day and stay warm. And don't slip on any more ice," Gideon said as he walked out the door.

As they rode away, Gideon said, "They already married off Charlotte. I hoped we'd have some time and maybe get a chance to get her back."

"Damn it. This is a sad day all around," Finnie said.

"Her father-in-law has a busted lip. I'd put money on it that Theo Sullenger gave it to him. Our good pastor was wearing a hand carved cross made out of green wood. It looked new enough that it probably still feels wet to the touch. He lost his old one when they killed Roy and Sissy for sure," Gideon said.

"Mary and I might be next on their list," Finnie mused.

"I thought of that too," Gideon said.

"We might have to keep an eye on them the next time bad weather looks to be coming in," Finnie said.

"That we might. We certainly don't have anything to arrest them with right now," Gideon said.

# Chapter 21

The scream in the middle of the night startled Finnie so badly that he nearly pissed himself. He felt for the matches on the nightstand and quickly lit the oil lamp. Mary sat up in bed holding her stomach. Her skin looked pale and her face etched in pain.

"Finnie, somethings wrong. My stomach hurts so bad," Mary said.

"I'm going to go get Doc right now," Finnie said before jumping out of bed and pulling on his trousers.

Mary threw back the covers, revealing a pool of blood between her legs. "Oh, God, I think I'm losing the baby."

Finnie ran out of the saloon and across the street. He slipped and fell in the snow, landing hard before gathering himself and jogging down to the doctor's office. Pounding on the door and hollering, the seconds seemed like hours as he waited. A lamp soon illuminated through the glass and Doc opened the door in his nightshirt.

"Finnie, what is it?" Doc asked as he rubbed his eye and noticed the snow caked on his friend's clothing.

"Mary's bad. Her stomach hurts and she's hemorrhaging. There's a lot of blood," Finnie said.

A moment passed as the doctor deciphered what the Irishman had said in his rapid-fire Irish accent. "Oh, good God. Get back to her and I'll throw some clothes on and get right over."

Mary lay clutching her stomach and moaning as Doc entered the bedroom. She gazed up at him and her eyes looked glassy.

"Doc, I hurt bad," she cried out.

"I'm here now. Let me have a look," the doctor said as he pulled the cover back.

The pool of blood looked significant, but he told himself that he had seen worse. He removed her undergarment, finding a small piece of tissue in the material and that her hemorrhaging still continued.

"Am I losing the baby?" Mary asked.

"I'm sorry, but yes, you are losing the baby. Sometimes nature aborts damaged fetuses. You're still young and can try again," Doc said solemnly.

Mary let out a scream of pain. "Why does it hurt so much?" she whimpered.

"Your body is in upheaval and it causes pain. I'm going to give you some laudanum to ease it," Doc said, reaching into his bag and producing a bottle of the syrup.

After taking two spoonfuls of the drug, Mary asked, "Am I going to die?"

"No, you're going to be fine. Where would I drink beer and spread gossip if I didn't have you and the Last Chance?" Doc said.

The laudanum kicked in and Mary's eyes slowly drifted shut. The doctor grabbed his stethoscope and checked her breathing and heartbeat while she slept. Satisfied that both sounded good, he sat back and waited.

"How bad is it, Doc?" Finnie asked.

The Irishman had been sitting so quietly in the corner that the doctor had forgotten about him. Doc looked over and for the first time since he met Finnie, his friend looked vulnerable and helpless. A lump formed in the doctor's throat and he walked over and placed his hand on Finnie's shoulder.

"She's still strong, but I tell you, she's losing too much blood. To be honest, I'm concerned," Doc said.

"Doc, you've got to save her. She's all I got," Finnie said.

"I'm doing my best. You know that. We're a long ways from that," Doc said.

By three o'clock in the morning, the doctor decided he needed to take action. The bleeding had failed to slow. Mary still slept and he awakened her to give her two more spoonfuls of laudanum. She seemed to be in a fog and said nothing as the doctor explained what he intended to do to her.

Waiting until Mary fell back to sleep, Doc removed two dilators and a curette from his bag along with carbolic acid and a clean towel. First, he washed his hands with the acid and then liberally doused the instruments with the same. Inserting the smaller of the dilators into her, he worked to open her cervix wider. After he completed this procedure, he manipulated the larger dilator into place until satisfied that the opening to the cervix was expanded to his satisfaction. Mary's only physical reaction was to rapidly blink her eyes. Picking up the curette, he looked the instrument over and inhaled a large breath before beginning his task. Maneuvering the instrument into the uterus, he carefully scraped the walls clean. Mary opened her eyes, but appeared oblivious to the intrusion to her body. As Doc removed the curette, tissue and thick blood oozed out with the tool.

Finnie started gagging and ran out into the hall to catch his breath. He eventually returned, pale in color, and dropped into a chair and as if exhausted.

"Finnie, I've done all I can do. The bleeding needs to coagulate or she's going to bleed to death. All we can do now is keep her comfortable and wait," Doc said and sat down beside the Irishman.

"How grave is it right now?" Finnie asked.

"I'll know more in a little while. We'll see if the procedure begins to help," Doc said.

"Why would this happen to Mary? She has a heart bigger than us two put together," Finnie lamented.

A little while later, Doc checked Mary's breathing and heart again before checking the bleeding. "She's holding her own and the bleeding might be a little slower," he said. "We might as well get some rest for a couple of hours."

The two men dozed off in chairs set side by side and slept for the next couple of hours until awakened by Mary calling out her dead husband's name.

"Eugene, Eugene, where are you?" Mary called out.

Finnie jumped up and leaned over his wife-to-be. "How are you feeling?" he asked.

"Eugene, I wondered where you were. Where's our baby?" she asked.

"It's asleep in the other room. You need to rest before you hold it," Finnie said.

"Her name is Claire. Quit calling her an it," Mary chided.

Doc stood beside Finnie watching Mary. Her eyes had gone from glassy to dull and lifeless and she was clearly delusional.

"Mary, I need to listen to your heart and breathing," Doc said as he placed his stethoscope on her chest.

After he finished, he pulled the blankets back to examine her.

"You just want a free peek at my privates. Back in my whoring days, I always wondered if you were too cheap or too old to have a go with me," Mary said.

The doctor smiled at her, but said nothing. She quickly drifted back to sleep and he walked to the window and looked out as dawn settled onto the town.

Finnie walked up beside the doctor. "How is she?' he asked.

"She's still bleeding too much and her breathing and heart have begun to weaken. She's not good. Finnie, this is your decision, but I think if I were you I would go find Gideon as soon as he gets in and have him go get Ethan, Sarah, and Abby. Mary needs all the friends that she has right now," Doc said.

"You think she's going to die, don't you?" Finnie asked.

The doctor took a big breath and rubbed his chin. "I never give up on one of my patients until they've breathed their last breath, but if that bleeding does not stop, she is in real trouble."

Tears spilled out of the eyes of the stout Irishman and he bit his lip as silent sobs racked his body, shaking his whole frame. Doc put his arm around Finnie's shoulders, but could think of nothing to say. They stayed standing there until the doctor's exhaustion got the better of him and he sat down in a chair. Finnie remained stationed at the window until he saw Gideon ride by a half-hour later. Grabbing his hat and coat, he walked out of the room.

Gideon stood lighting the stove in the jail. "Good morning my sawed-off little -," he said before stopping. "What's the matter?"

"Mary lost the baby and she's bad. Doc thought that I should ask you to go get Ethan, Sarah, and Abby. He says she needs all the friends that she has," Finnie said.

Finnie stood in front of Gideon looking smaller than normal and as helpless as a little boy lost in the woods. At a loss on how to comfort his friend, Gideon stood awkwardly frozen in place. Thoughts of losing Mary made him physically weak and he wanted to take a seat.

"I'm sorry, Finnie. Don't give up. Mary's a fighter," Gideon said as he walked over and placed a hand on Finnie's shoulder.

"Life's not fair, and for people like Mary, they bear more than their fair share of the burden," Finnie said.

"I know. I'm going to get going so that I can get back," Gideon said.

Riding first to see Joann, Gideon dispatched her to go watch Chance. He then headed to Ethan's cabin. Upon hearing the news, Ethan and Sarah left immediately for town. Zack would remain behind to be on hand for Benjamin's return from school. Finally, Gideon rode to his cabin. Abby had already saddled her horse after Joann had arrived with the news and the couple rode to town.

Ethan and Sarah stood at the foot of the bed with Finnie standing between them as Gideon and Abby entered the bedroom. Finnie looked as if he would melt away if not for the two people standing shoulder to shoulder against him to prop him up. Doc sat in a chair at Mary's bedside taking her pulse. She had just gone back to sleep after having given a lively talk interspersed with lucid thoughts and moments of shear confusion. Gideon looked down at Mary and could not get over the fact that she looked so young and helpless. She didn't look much older than Joann did. All of the spirit that had marched her on through a tragic life looked to be fading away.

"How is she?" Gideon asked as he pulled off his hat.

"The hemorrhaging won't stop and she's getting weaker. She's in God's hands now. There's nothing more that I can do," Doc answered.

Ethan cleared his throat. "Why don't we make a semi-circle around her and hold hands while I say a prayer."

The group of six surrounded the bed and grasped hands.

"Dear Father in Heaven, Mary lies before us sick and in need of your blessings. She is one of the people that makes Last Stand the special place that it is. She may even be the heart of Last Stand and her friends and Finnie are not ready to turn her over to you. We ask that you restore her health and let her live to bring her joy to this world. I know that Heaven would be a richer place with her, but we need this angel in Last Stand. Dear God, I beg you to restore Mary's health. Amen," Ethan said.

Mary's eyes opened and she trained them on Gideon. "Gideon, what are you doing in my bedroom? You'd better not be here for a poke. We can't do that anymore. You know that you broke my heart, but it's okay now. I came to realize that we were just supposed to be friends. You and Abby were meant to be together and I don't know why, but somehow, someway, Finnie and I were meant to be together too. I love that little Irishman," she said before fading back to sleep.

A mournful sound of grief escaped from Gideon and he looked around the room in embarrassment. A flood of sorrow washed over him so great that he could not contain it and he ran from the room as uncontrollable crying broke free.

Abby followed him out of the room. Her husband had his face smashed against the hall wall and he pounded it with his fists like a toddler throwing a fit as he blubbered indecipherably. In all the years that she had known Gideon, she had never witnessed such an outbreak of shear grief from him. Deciding that it was best to let him get it all out, she waited patiently for him to release all of the pent-up emotion exploding from him.

Gideon finally turned around, using the wall for support to keep himself propped up. He gulped large breaths of air as if suffocating and his finger tingled from hyperventilating. Once able to speak, he said, "Abby, you know that you're the love of my life. I need you more than anything, but I need Mary in my life too. Back when I returned to Last Stand all shot up and mad at the world, everybody here that cared for me, cared for me because of who I once was except for Sarah and Mary. Those two cared for me even at my worst and because of who they thought I could be without ever having known the old me. I can't tell you how much that meant to me. Here were two people that probably should have thought that I was a lost cause, but they didn't. They gave me a reason to believe in myself again. To this day, they make me want to be a better man. I don't know what I'll do if I don't have Mary there."

Abby placed a hand on each of Gideon's shoulders. Her eyes brimmed with tears and in a measured voice, she said, "Here's what you are going to do. Mary never gave up on you and you're not going to give up on her. You have to believe in her strength to survive. You have no other choice."

Hugging his wife, Gideon said, "I don't know why life has to be so hard."

"I guess it's to make us appreciate the good times. Let's get back in there," Abby said.

Using the back of his hands, Gideon wiped his eyes as they walked into the room. Everyone sat in chairs that Finnie had retrieved before they had all arrived. All of their faces looked lined with either tension or exhaustion. Mary slept, her breathing shallow and barely audible.

"Any change?" Gideon asked.

Doc shook his head no.

Delta took it upon herself to open the saloon and run it. She brought food on a tray up to the bedroom after the lunch crowd had thinned. As the others ate, she leaned down over Mary and whispered, "Don't you dare leave me. We've been through way too much together for you to go off and leave me on my own. I need you." She then ran out of the room without another word.

Mary awoke late in the afternoon. She opened her eyes to see Abby and Sarah sitting on either side of her. Glancing back and forth between the two of them, she used only her eyes as if too weak to move her head.

"Did you see Claire? Isn't she a beautiful baby? I need to nurse -," Mary whispered before her eyes closed and her head fell to the side.

Abby let out a scream and jumped up. Doc moved quickly to his patient and grabbed her wrist to take her pulse.

"Is she gone?" Finnie asked quietly from the foot of the bed as if afraid to hear his own words

"No, she passed out from lack of blood," Doc said.

The doctor dug out his stethoscope from his bag and listened to Mary's chest. He moved the instrument all over as he checked her breathing and heartbeat. At the doctor's request, Sarah and Abby held the blanket up to protect Mary's privacy from the men as he examined her.

"The bleeding has finally almost stopped. I wouldn't consider it significant any longer, but at this point, she's very weak. Her breathing is shallow and her heartbeat is no longer strong. Mary has lost a tremendous amount of blood. She could pull through this, but it'll take a miracle. Usually they just keep getting weaker at this point," Doc said before collapsing in a chair, seemingly resigned to the inevitable.

Color came to Sarah's cheeks and she jumped up from her chair as if headed out the door before spinning around and facing the room. Her hand shot up and her boney finger shook at the others in the room. "Nobody in this room is going to give up on Mary. If you are, then you might as well go home. If she doesn't have the strength to go on, we will be her strength. Everybody needs to keep praying and willing her to live. We all know that Benjamin would have died when he was kidnapped if not for Mary. She was there for us and we can't lose hope for her now. There's no way in hell that I'm letting her go without a fight," she said before walking over to Mary and taking her hand. A look of determination so fierce that it would have been comical in another setting came over her as she willed Mary to live.

Finally, to break the awkward silence, Finnie said, "Doc, the next room is empty. Why don't you go get some rest? You're exhausted. We can keep watch over her and get you if you're needed."

"I think I will. I'm not as young as I used to be," the doctor said before shuffling out of the room.

At dinnertime, the two couples took turns going to the hotel for a meal. Finnie refused to leave Mary's side and Ethan and Sarah brought back some food that he forced himself to eat. Doc arose at close to eight o'clock and returned to the bedroom looking remarkably refreshed for a man of his age. His eyes looked clear and his step had regained its vitality. He checked Mary again and announced that her condition had neither improved nor worsened. His belly growled and he remarked that he was starving. He then left to find John and have dinner.

The vigilance kept on through the night. Eventually, each person gave in to sleep and took a turn in the other bedroom. Even Finnie finally gave in to his exhaustion and took a nap. Mary never regained consciousness throughout the night, and before morning, they all dozed in their chairs.

Everyone remained asleep as the sunshine flooded through the window and melting snow dripped from the roof looking like a shower of diamonds as they passed. Mary opened her eyes and watched the spectacle on the other side of the glass as she tried to gather her thoughts. She looked around the crowded room at the sleeping bodies positioned in the most awkward poses imaginable and wondered if they were here for her deathwatch. Death didn't seem out of the question. She had to summon all her stamina just to turn her head. "Hey," she called out as loud as her strength allowed.

Gideon and Finnie opened their eyes immediately. Their years of war had taught them to be alert to noise as they slept. Finnie shot out of his chair and moved to Mary's side as the others stirred from the commotion.

Taking Mary's hand, Finnie asked, "How are you feeling?"

In a weak voice, she asked, "Am I dying?"

"I would say not. Nobody here would allow it," Finnie said with a smile.

"I feel like it," Mary whispered as a circle of people surrounded her.

"Let me have some room," Doc grumbled as he tried to get the stethoscope to Mary's chest.

Everyone remained quiet as the doctor listened for fear of enduring his wrath. As Doc pulled the instrument out of his ears, he said, "Mary, you're very weak, but better than you were or have a right to be," he said.

"Look at all of you here for me. You all look like I feel," Mary said, making everyone smile.

Doc turned to Abby and Sarah. "She needs milk, calf liver, and greens. Do you girls think that you can make that happen?"

Mary made a face.

"Young lady, this is serious. You need to eat whether you feel like it or not. Food is the only thing that is going to make you better. You have no idea how sick you are," Doc said.

Gideon ushered everyone away from the bed. "Let's all get out of here and let Finnie and Mary have some time alone while the girls rustle her up some food."

As they walked out the door, they could hear Mary ask Finnie, "I lost our baby, didn't I?"

"Yes, but we about lost you too. We can talk when you're stronger," Finnie said.

Mary closed her eyes to rest, but not before a single tear escaped down her cheek.

# Chapter 22

Recovery for Mary proved slow going. Abby, Sarah, and Joann took turns caring for her as she continued to recuperate. Her appetite remained good, but her spirit low. She spoke very little and made for poor company, causing the women to give up on conversation and concentrate on knitting and sewing. Another bout of confusion sent Doc scrambling to check on her, but he found no signs of new hemorrhaging and the episode quickly passed.

Finnie hovered over Mary as much as his job allowed and his constant attention got on her last nerve. Though she tried to conceal her feelings, a part of her resented Finnie for impregnating her. She reasoned that if she hadn't been pregnant, she would have never gotten her hopes up for raising a child or nearly have died. Having relations again with Finnie seemed like something that she could not even fathom.

Six days after losing the baby, she still remained bedridden. Sarah tried to carry on a conversation with her, but found her unreceptive to small talk. While sympathetic to her plight, Sarah sized up the situation and realized that the time had come for a heart-to-heart talk.

"Mary, we need to talk. Nobody around here realizes what you are going through better than I do. I lived through three miscarriages. I never got as sick as you did, but I felt like I died inside on each one. There were days where I didn't think I could go on, especially after the last one. They all took some time to get over, but I eventually did. Even though it doesn't feel like it now, time will heal you. Do you understand?" Sarah said as she looked into Mary's eyes to see if she were listening.

"I guess, but this doesn't feel like something that you ever get over," Mary said.

"I know it doesn't and I'm not saying that you should get over it in a day or two, I'm just saying that you will get over this. I'll tell you something else that I've never told a soul, certainly not Ethan, not even Abby, but there were times when I resented Ethan. I needed somebody to blame and he was the logical choice. He was the one that helped make the baby inside of me. That passed in time too. A miscarriage is probably nature's way of ridding us of a baby that would not have survived anyway. I tried reminding myself of that on the bad days," Sarah said.

"Sometimes I feel as if life likes to kick me around. Did you know that I was resenting Finnie?" Mary asked.

"No, I just figured that if I felt that way that maybe you were too and I wanted you to know that it will pass," Sarah answered.

"Thank you. Getting over this seems like a long time away," Mary said as her eyes welled with tears.

"I know it does, but it's time to get out of bed. We are going to walk the hall," Sarah said.

"Sarah, I don't think I'm strong enough," Mary protested.

"Yes, you are. I can tolerate your grieving, but I can't tolerate you lying around withering away. I owe you too much to let you get by with that. Come on. Get up. I'm not asking, I'm telling. You've laid around long enough," Sarah said and started tugging on Mary's arm.

Deciding that now was not the time to provoke Sarah, Mary arose reluctantly and unsteadily to her feet. The loss of blood made her lightheaded and she swayed while still in the clutches of Sarah. Her head cleared somewhat as her body adjusted to being vertical and after taking a couple of breaths. They headed out the door and down the hall. Mary's steps were small and slow. She could have been mistaken for an elderly lady as she moved. The walking felt exhausting but a glance at Sarah's face banished any hope of abandoning the stroll. Sarah insisted that she make three trips down the corridor before allowing her to go back to bed.

"We're going to walk on the hour, every hour, for the rest of the day," Sarah announced.

Mary managed a smile for the first time since losing the baby. "You really are as mean as Ethan says you are," she joked.

Finnie came to check on Mary at noon and found her turning her nose up at another meal of liver. She smiled at him before turning her attention back to the bite of food and trying to marshal her resolve to eat it.

"Death may have been preferable to one more bite of liver," Mary said.

"I would imagine that you've had your fill of that stuff. How are you feeling?" Finnie said.

Sarah stood. "I'm going to take a break and get something to eat," she said on her way out the door.

"I'm better. Sarah made me get up and walk. We've done it twice so far. She's bossy when she wants to be," Mary said begrudgingly.

"I can still hear you," Sarah hollered from the hall and made the couple laugh.

"I'm glad to hear it. Your color is better today," Finnie remarked.

"I'm sorry I haven't felt much like talking. I've just been so blue," she said.

"It's to be expected. I haven't felt like cutting a rug myself," he said.

"I know this has been hard on you too. We both wanted this baby, but we'll get through it. It's just going to take some time," she said. Her words lacked conviction, but she repeated what Sarah had said with the assumption that her friend knew what she was talking about.

"Well, time is the one thing that I hope that we have plenty of," Finnie said and smiled at her.

"Me too. Sarah lost three babies before they had Benjamin. There's still hope," she said.

"As long as I have you, I'll be fine either way," Finnie said and leaned over and kissed her – liver breath and all.

"Do you still want to go ahead and get married or do you want to wait and see if we have a baby?" Mary asked.

"Of course, I want to marry you. I wanted to marry you before I knew about a baby. I just wasn't very good at going about it," Finnie said.

"I still want to get married too," Mary said. Knowing that Sarah had resented Ethan had somehow already lessened her resentment of Finnie. She did love him and knew that there really was nobody to blame for the loss of the baby.

"Finish your meal," Finnie cajoled.

Forcing down her last bite of liver, Mary said, "Will you move my tray? I need a nap before Sarah gets back and makes me walk again."

After removing the tray, Finnie kissed Mary again. "I'll see you this evening," he said before leaving.

As Finnie walked out of the saloon, he spied Doc and John walking down the street towards him and waited for their arrival.

"What are you two outlaws up to?" Finnie asked.

"We had our picture made," John said enthusiastically.

"All the better for your wanted poster," Finnie teased.

"How is Mary today?" John asked.

"More like herself. Sarah got her up and walking," Finnie said.

Doc let out a chuckle. "Leave it to Sarah to light the fire," he said. "We're going to have lunch. Care to join us?"

"No, I've already eaten. I need to get back to the jail. You two are beginning to look like two peas in a pod," Finnie said.

The father and son smiled and said nothing before crossing the street to the hotel.

Gideon sat at his desk as Finnie walked in. The sheriff seemed distracted and barely aware that his deputy had entered the room. He made for poor company lately. The troubles with Paradise and Jack's death weighed heavily on him. Mary's sickness had been the final straw in souring his disposition.

After giving Gideon an update on Mary, Finnie said, "Why don't you go home early? Get your mind off things for a while. Maybe starting fresh tomorrow will help."

Sitting back in his chair, Gideon rubbed his scar before running his hand through his hair. "I think you're right. I'm not getting anything done here anyway."

"I do have some other news. I was having lunch at the saloon and I sat down with that bootmaker, Otis Daniel, and he told me that Pastor Gordon paid him a visit. He said the pastor told them that since the death of his father and his taking over the church that he wanted to get to know more of the citizens of Last Stand and he'd like to come in and talk to him and his wife. They let him in and things were going well until he asked them if they were married in the eyes of the Lord. When they told him that the justice of the peace had married them, the pastor went into a rant about their unholy matrimony. They made him leave," Finnie said.

"Really? I guess that helps prove our theory. So, not only are common-law marriages a sin, but so are marriages by the justice of the peace. Next thing you know, only marriages that Gordon officiated will be deemed holy. I think I'll go home on that note," Gideon said as he arose from his seat. "I'll see you tomorrow. Tell Mary I expect her to be serving me a beer in short order."

With fall well underway, the sun was positioned much farther to the south. Gideon always liked the way that the light hit the trees this time of year, making interesting contrast with the shadows. Most of the trees were now bare of leaves and stood stark against the backdrop of mountains. The air felt cool on the skin and winter would soon be in full force. Fall tended to make him melancholy anyway with its reminder of another year coming to an end. He arrived home feeling as solemn as he had departing from Last Stand.

"What brings you home so early?" Abby asked as he walked into the cabin.

"Finnie's idea. I think I depressed him," Gideon said as he hung up his hat and sat down at the table.

"Don't talk too loudly. Chance is taking his nap. Well, nobody could mistake you for the life of the party, that's for sure. Do you want to talk about it?" Abby said.

"I don't know what there's to talk about. Jack would still be alive if not for me, Mary about died, and I know the people responsible for the hangings but I can't prove it," Gideon said.

"We've already talked about Jack. He chose to ride with you and bad things happened. It's nothing new. He certainly wouldn't have blamed you and you shouldn't either. And Mary didn't die. You should be thankful that she's alive. It's sad the baby died, but Mary is getting better by the day. I certainly didn't think we would be saying that. I thought we would lose her. And you'll catch the men that did the hangings. You always do. I don't know why you doubt yourself," she said.

"Still doesn't seem like much to be happy about," he said.

Abby sat down in Gideon's lap. "You know the answer to that. Happiness doesn't have anything to do with what's going on around you. It's merely a choice on how to handle those things. Just like when you came back here and decided to make a new life for yourself. Your past didn't change. Just your way of handling it did."

Gideon smiled at his wife. Her wisdom had left him defenseless. "How did I pick somebody as smart as you?" he asked.

"You didn't. I picked you when I was about fourteen years old. You're lucky I'm a patient person," she said and kissed him.

"You have all the answers today," Gideon said.

"If you carry me to the bedroom I'll have an answer to putting an even bigger smile on your face," she said.

# Chapter 23

Eggs were frying in the skillet and the smell of bacon permeated the air. Zack sat at the table trying to shake off his drowsiness. Joann had roused him early to spend all of Saturday working on their homestead. Gideon and Ethan had helped him finish the well and now Joann seemed hell-bent on getting her husband to fell all the trees necessary for building the cabin. They had already borrowed Ethan's wagon the night before and she planned to haul off the dirt pile at the well while he chopped down trees.

"How many more trees do you think we'll need?" Joann asked as she flipped the eggs.

"I don't have a clue. A lot more than we have now. I'll have to get Gideon or Ethan to help me figure out that," Zack answered.

"Do you think you'll have enough by spring?" she further inquired.

"I'm not much good at reading the future. It'll depend on the weather and things. It takes a lot of time cutting all the branches off the trunks once the tree is down," he said.

"I can't wait to move into our new home. Aren't you excited?" Joann said as she placed the two plates onto the table and sat down to eat.

"Yes, but this is a good cabin that Ethan provides for us. We could be doing a lot worse," Zack said.

"I know, but I can't make this into our own home. There'd be no point in it. We can have some nice things with that money," Joann waxed on.

"Don't forget that we'll have plenty of things to buy to run the homestead. We can't borrow things forever. We're going to need a plow and an ox or mule to pull it. I think we could make good money selling hay to the other ranchers," Zack said.

"Zackary Barlow, I'm aware of that. You're getting to be slab-sided. You could have a little fun and dream with me," Joann said.

Feeling slighted by her remark, he pulled off a bite of bacon. "I'm still fun. You're not the one working all week and then cutting trees on Saturday. If you're so worried about fun, we could've done something besides work today."

Joann smiled over the top of her coffee cup. "You're just sore that it's too cold to skinny dip now. I bet you'd be out that door by now if you thought that was going to happen."

Unable to keep from smiling, Zack said, "If my memory serves me well, it was you that was the first one into the water."

"That's true, but when I started it, I didn't know that we were going to have to cool down just about every time we worked," Joann retorted.

"I don't remember having to twist your arm," Zack replied.

"How many babies do you hope we have?" she asked.

"I don't know. I guess how many God sees fit for us to have. They're nothing I'm in a hurry to start having," Zack said.

"Well, you'd never know it by your actions. You know when you play with fire all the time that you'll eventually get burned," Joann said.

"Listen to you. You're a fine one to talk," Zack said before gulping down his last bite of egg.

"True, but I'm not worried about the consequences. I'm ready for a baby whenever it happens. Let's get out of here before all this talk gives you the itch," Joann said smugly.

∞

Doc's last patient of the day walked out of the office and John entered the room when he heard the front door shut. The two men planned to have dinner at the hotel on John's last night in town. In the morning, he was scheduled to catch the stagecoach.

The doctor walked over to a cabinet and pulled out a small drawer. "Here's the bullet I retrieved out of you. It should be good for pulling out of your pocket at a pub and telling your story. Might even be good for a free drink or two," he said as he placed the lead in his son's hand.

"I imagine it will impress the boys. Kate might not think much of it," John said as he bounced the bullet in his hand to feel its weight.

"I made sure that the hotel has elk meat. Mary getting sick sure put a damper on the get-together and Ethan hasn't shot an elk yet. I wish you could've had some meat that Sarah prepared. She's the best cook around these here parts," Doc said.

"At least I'll get to taste it. I'm just glad Mary is doing better. She means a lot to you, doesn't she?" John said.

"That she does. She's had a hard life and she keeps right on going with her best foot forward. There are not many people that can do that. She's makes us all better people, I think," Doc said.

"That is a rare quality. Father, you are a lucky man to have such an eclectic cast of characters to call friends. I'm going to have so many stories to tell. I could keep people in stitches all night with Finnie's escapades alone," John said as he slipped the bullet into his pocket.

Until that moment, John had avoided addressing his father by title. Doc's heartbeat quickened and the hairs on his neck stood on end. His eyes moistened and he hugged his son out of a need to hold him and to avoid his embarrassment. He could now go to his grave knowing he had been addressed by the one title he gave up on ever hearing years ago.

"I'm so glad that you came to see me. I do not possess the words to tell you what it means to me to have finally met my son and seeing you proved more wonderful than my wildest dreams could have ever imagined. If only your mother and I could live our lives all over, but that's a waste of time to dwell on. Let's go eat. I'm hungry," Doc said as he wiped his eyes with the back of his sleeve.

The two men walked to the hotel and ordered their meals. As they waited for their food, John said, "Getting to know you has been more than I could have hoped for too. I was scared to death to meet you. I'm so proud to see the life my father has carved out for himself out here. You're so much a part of the fabric that makes up Last Stand. This place is harsh and primitive, but its beauty and its people are intoxicating. I can see why you made Last Stand your home."

'It sure can get into an easterner's blood, that's for sure," Doc said.

"Well, I can say that it's gotten into mine. Speaking of blood, do you think I favor you?" John asked.

"Maybe around the eyes, but you have your Grandfather Hamilton's nose and chin. You favor the rich side of your family," Doc said with a laugh.

"Mother always thought I looked like Grandfather, but since she would never even acknowledge that I had a father, I guess she couldn't say that I looked like you," John said.

"Your mother was something back in the day. We would go to a dance and all eyes would turn to her. And she was so funny. We used to laugh all the time. She could find humor in just about anything," Doc said.

"Well, you must have taken her humor with you when you left. Not to say that she was unkind or a bad mother, but funny would not be a word I would use to describe her," John said.

"I hate to hear that. Life can steal our soul if we let it. It's certainly not for the faint-hearted," Doc said and seemed to get lost in thought.

"You must promise me to come see the family," John said to snap his father out of his musings.

"I'll try, but you have to understand that I'm the only doctor in these here parts. The people need me. I don't know if I could be gone that long," Doc said.

"Father, I only ask that you try to make it happen. I'll do my best to talk Kate into coming, but I fear that will be a hard sell," John said.

"Especially, since you went and got yourself shot. Kate will be thinking that outlaws walk down the street shooting people willy-nilly. She might not appreciate you consorting in a saloon either," Doc said as the food was placed on the table.

"I'm sure not going to tell her about what goes on upstairs," John said with a laugh.

"Those days are about over. As soon as Mary figures out how to get Delta out of it, it'll be over. She doesn't have the stomach to let it go on much longer," Doc said.

John took his first bite of the meat, chewing it slowly. "It does taste pretty much like beef, but I can definitely tell that it's wild game."

"I don't know how she does it, but Sarah can get out most of that wild taste. That's why I wanted you to eat her cooking. At least you can say that you tried it," Doc said.

"Maybe on my next trip Gideon can teach me how to shoot a gun," John said.

Doc laughed. "Well, you already started dressing like him. You're at least half-way there."

"I can't wait to see Kate's reaction when I wear those clothes around the house. She'll probably cut me down like back in the old days when she was a waitress," John said.

"You never know. The ladies love the cowboys," Doc said and winked at John, provoking a loud laugh and a slap of the table from his son.

# Chapter 24

The bright warm morning quickly faded as clouds rolled in and the wind kicked up out of the northwest. The temperature dropped dramatically in two hours' time and people that had been walking the streets of Last Stand in jackets could now be seen bundled up in heavy coats. Gideon stoked the fire in the jail's stove to knock the chill out of the room as Finnie slipped in from a check of the town.

"The stage should be headed out in a few minutes. We best get out there and tell John goodbye. I need to go get Mary. She wants to try to see him off," Finnie said.

"Is she ready for that?" Gideon asked as he pulled on his coat.

"I think so. She's a lot better. Sarah did wonders for her," Finnie said.

"Sarah has a way of doing that. She's not one to be trifled with. Make sure you get her good and wrapped up," Gideon warned.

"Yes, dear. I would've never thought of that," Finnie said as headed out the door.

Gideon waited by the stagecoach as Finnie came with Mary. She wore a winter coat with a blanket draped over her head. The Irishman held her arm as they walked though she appeared to be steady on her feet, but slow in step. The cold brought color to her cheeks and she smiled at Gideon.

"You're looking much improved," Gideon said.

"That I am. There'll be no foot races any time soon, but I have Finnie to jump at my every whim," Mary said.

"That's what I like to keep him doing too," Gideon said.

Doc and John joined them. John had purchased a new ranch coat that morning after the temperature began dropping and he wore it along with his new western attire. He looked like a rancher leaving on a trip.

"I think we made a cowboy out of you," Gideon said as he shook John's hand.

"These clothes beat wearing a suit any day of the week," John remarked.

Finnie and Gideon said their goodbyes before Mary gave John a hug and a kiss on the cheek.

"You've made Doc very happy and that makes me very happy. Have a safe trip," she said.

"Young lady, you need to get back inside the saloon. I've doctored you enough for a while," Doc said as passengers began boarding.

Finnie wrapped his arm around Mary and began escorting her back to the saloon.

"Father, even taking a bullet proved worth it to have finally met you. Write us plenty of letters. Until we meet again, know that I love you," John said and shook his father's hand.

The doctor pulled his son to him and gave him a hug. "God's speed. I love you too. Tell your family that I look forward to meeting them."

With John's trunk loaded, he took one final look and climbed aboard. The other passengers were already seated and the stagecoach took off, leaving Gideon and Doc to watch it disappear down the street.

"Are you going to be okay?" Gideon asked.

"Of course, I am. Don't think that I'm going to go soft and start buying all the beers for you. You'd probably try to take advantage of the situation if you got the chance," Doc said and walked away towards his office.

Gideon smiled watching the old doctor shuffle away. The sheriff crossed the street, walking into the jail and finding it now warm.

Finnie stood at the stove clapping his hands together. "I'd hate to take a piss out there right now. It'd blow twenty feet and be frozen by the time it hit the ground."

"Well, I got a job for you so you better take a piss before you go. I need you to ride to Ethan's place and get Zack. Make sure he gets some warm clothing. We're going to be freezing our ass off today," Gideon said.

In exasperation, Finnie asked, "What are we going to do and why can't you go get him?"

"We're going to go watch Paradise. They might try to hang somebody with the snow coming in and if they do, I aim to put an end to it. We could use an extra gun. And I'm pulling rank on you for going to get Zack. There are some perks to being sheriff," Gideon said with a smile.

"You're a hard-hearted man, Gideon Johann. You ought to be ashamed of yourself for taking advantage of your subordinate. A true leader goes before his men," Finnie whined.

"I'll give that some thought while I warm myself by the fire," Gideon said.

Finnie tugged his hat down tight and left without saying another word. By the time he returned with Zack, flurries floated to the ground and their hats and coats were speckled with snow. The two men pulled off their gloves and quickly walked to the fire with arms outstretched.

Gideon got up from his desk. "You two grab a couple of boxes of cartridges off my desk. I want to be prepared," he said as he grabbed his coat off its peg.

"I don't see how three of us are going to be able to keep an eye on them and not get spotted," Finnie said as he continued to warm himself.

"For one, we're not dealing with Jesse James here. They're not exactly professional outlaws. And second is arrogance. Pastor Gordon's self-righteousness will have him convinced that he is protected by God in his mission," Gideon said before opening the door. "Let's get this over with."

"You only let me be your deputy when there's a chance to get killed. I think you must have a death wish for me so that your daughter can get a new man," Zack said.

"Yeah, like I want to hear her wailing and blaming me," Gideon said.

"Well, thank you for that warm sentiment," Zack said.

"I might become Mary's bartender before this is done. I can think of warmer things to do," Finnie grumbled.

Zack said, "I thought that you already were her little helper."

"Boy, I was the one that taught you to box and I can still whip you any day of the week. I should move back to Ireland. You know, we don't have snakes there," Finnie said.

As they mounted their horses, Gideon said, "I think that you just got compared to a snake. Finnie's a little testy since he's sleeping in the spare bedroom while Mary recovers, if you know what I mean."

"Actually, I was talking about the both of you. You can tease about Mary now, but I saw you crying like a baby when you were worried about her," Finnie said.

Gideon never showed a reaction to Finnie's remark, but out of the corner of his eye, he could see Zack looking at him in surprise. "That I did. She scared me. None of us could stand to lose Mary," he said as he nudged Buck down the street.

The wind had slackened off some, but the trip still made for a miserable ride. The snowfall picked up momentum as they rode, causing the men to pull their hats low and crouch in the saddle. Nobody spoke as they traveled. Before the church came into view, they cut off from the road and angled behind a timber where they tied the horses.

"You two can stay here. I'll walk through the woods and see what's going on," Gideon said as he retrieved his spyglass from the saddlebag and pulled his Winchester from its scabbard.

The woods provided an easy walk. The trees were mature and had shaded out most of the undergrowth and a deer trail cut through it. Snow was just starting to stick in the path. Gideon's belly growled and he wished they had eaten lunch before heading out. As he reached the end of the timber, he crouched behind a tree and peeked around it. Five horses stood tied in front of the church and smoke rolled from the building's chimney. He watched for over a half-hour before five men walked out of the church. Through his spyglass, he could see Pastor Gordon, Mr. Hobbs, and the three other men. They all mounted their horses and headed west.

As Gideon returned to Finnie and Zack, he said, "They're up to no-good."

"Well, the good pastor has caught me on a day where I feel as mean as a miner with a pocketful of gold that finds the whorehouse went out of business and the saloon ran dry," Finnie said as he climbed aboard his horse.

Staying out of view, the three lawmen followed at a far enough distance to avoid detection. Just enough snow had accumulated to make following the tracks easy and without fear of losing their quarry. The Paradise men continued west before angling north. They avoided the road, choosing a course to avoid chancing someone catching sight of them.

The farther that Gideon trailed the men, the more his uneasiness grew. The hair on the back of his neck began to stand on end and he no longer noticed the cold. He contemplated announcing his fear, but wondered if he were paranoid and rode on without speaking.

"Gideon, they're headed for your place," Zack announced.

"That's what I'm beginning to fear," Gideon said.

"They have to know that you're not there," Finnie said.

"I imagine they were planning a welcome home surprise," Gideon said.

"What's your plan?" Finnie asked.

"They're still a good two miles from the cabin and I don't want to chance whether there's enough time to circle around and beat them. We'll double-time it until we get them in view. Once they spot us, we'll swoop in on them. If they're smart, they'll stop because there's not a damn law they've broken. If they run, we'll pursue and hope they veer away from the cabin. The moment that I know they're still headed towards my place, I'm opening fire. We can't let them get to the cabin and inside it. Unless one of you has a better idea?" Gideon said.

"That sounds as good as anything," Finnie said and kneed his horse into a trot.

A half-mile down the trail, they could see the five riders a quarter of a mile ahead. They continued after them in an easy trot. When they had closed to within a couple hundred yards, the lawmen were spotted. The Paradise men brought their horses to a stop and made a half-circle as they looked to be discussing their next move. They abruptly took off in a dead run with their pursuers in chase.

The horses of the Paradise men were not fast or conditioned and began to slow. Gideon began to pull away from Zack and Finnie and close in on the riders. Pulling his rifle from the scabbard, he rested the weapon across the saddle and hoped the men would change course. They continued on a straight line towards the cabin and Gideon calmly brought his Winchester up and took aim, gently squeezing the trigger. The shot missed and the riders hunkered down in the saddle and slapped their horses with the reins to coax more speed.

Gideon's cabin came into view and the realization sunk in that he couldn't stop the men from reaching his home. Hoping to alert Abby to the danger, he started taking quick aim and firing rapidly. Finnie and Zack lagged fifty yards behind him and they began firing in a desperate attempt to prevent the men from reaching their destination. One of the riders slumped forward in his saddle before falling off the side of the horse with his feet caught in the stirrups. The scared horse continued running and the man bounced against the ground in a macabre dance with the land.

Abby heard the gunfire and looked out the window. She could see the riders headed towards the cabin and ran to both of the doors, placing the four by four pieces of lumber across the entrances and into their metal arms. Chance played on the floor. She grabbed him and his toys and carried him to the loft where she blocked his exit. Returning downstairs, she retrieved the shotgun hung above the door, checking to make sure that the gun was loaded. She pulled a hammer back and waited.

The four remaining men reached the cabin and ran for the door. Finding the entrance barred, they ran for the cover of the trees in the yard as Gideon quickly advanced upon them at a dead run. Holding his empty rifle in his left hand, he drew his revolver and fired at the closest man. Mr. Hobbs let out an ear-piercing scream before toppling over. The others reached the trees and a barrage of shots forced Gideon to retreat to the tree line beside the barn where Finnie and Zack joined him.

"Thank God Abby barred the door," Gideon said.

"What now?" Zack asked.

"We'll get them to empty their guns. None of them carries side arms and I imagine that any extra cartridges that they had were in their saddlebags. Those horses are God knows where. They weren't exactly prepared for this," Gideon said.

Pastor Gordon yelled, "Sheriff, we are angels of the Lord that have come down to smitten you. Prepare to meet your Maker and to be cast into the bowels of Hell."

"I don't see any wings on you. I think you're just a murderer. Remember that sixth commandment about not killing. You're nothing more than a crazy hypocrite," Gideon hollered.

A single shot thudded into the tree that Gideon crouched behind, sending a chunk of bark flying. Zack quickly leaned around his tree and returned fire. A game of cat and mouse pot shots followed. Gideon checked his watch. Winnie would not be returning from school for over an hour. With Abby and Chance safe in the cabin, he remained content to let pastor and his men run out of bullets.

Moments later, the Paradise men began shooting rapidly and made returning fire nearly impossible. Gideon peeked around the tree just as Gordon disappeared behind the cabin.

"Gordon's going to try to get into the cabin," Gideon yelled as he stood. He took one step from behind the tree and felt the crushing weight of Zack tackling him to the ground.

"Gideon, that's suicide," Zack hollered as he dragged his father-in-law back behind the tree and held him in a bear hug.

"Damn it, Zack, let me go. That's my wife and son," Gideon screamed.

"You can't help them if you're dead," Zack protested.

The shooting paused and the sound of breaking glass cut through the silence. Gideon struggled in the grips of the much larger Zack, delivering painful elbows. The unmistakable roar of a shotgun blast shattered the momentary quiet.

"They're running," Finnie called out.

"Kill the son of a bitches," Gideon yelled as Zack released him.

Finnie squeezed off two rounds as Gideon and Zack scrambled to retrieve the rifles they'd lost in their scuffle.

"They're down," Finnie hollered.

Gideon took off in a dead run for the other side of the cabin with Finnie and Zack in close pursuit. Snow came down hard now and made it hard to see without getting pelted in the eyeballs. They reached the corner and slid to a stop. Pastor Gordon lay sprawled on the ground. His head had been obliterated by the shotgun blast. The snow peppered down on what had once been his face and dissolved into the red goo. Abby stood at the broken window looking out at the lifeless body.

"Abby, open the door," Gideon told her.

She remained standing at the window as if she hadn't heard and Gideon repeated himself. Slowly, she turned around and disappeared. He rushed around the cabin and stood waiting for her when the door opened, pulling her into his arms.

"Where's Chance?" Gideon asked.

"He's in the loft," Abby said in a monotone voice.

"I'll get him," Zack said as he maneuvered past the couple and through the door.

Chance sat on the floor playing with his toys as if nothing out of the ordinary had taken place. He smiled at Zack and held out his arms to be picked up. Zack happily obliged and returned the boy to his parents.

The sight of Chance broke the damn of emotion stored up in Abby and she began crying uncontrollably. Chance began crying too and Gideon tried his best to comfort the both of them.

"I had to shoot him," Abby said between sobs.

"Yes, you did. You saved Chance's life and ours too. That man was pure evil," Gideon said.

He continued to hold Abby until the crying was all out of her. By the time she stopped, Chance had cried himself to sleep in her arms.

"Why don't you go lie down with Chance? I want to get this cleaned up before Winnie gets home and there's not much time," Gideon said.

"Okay," Abby said. "Do you still think I'm a good person?"

"I think you're my hero," Gideon said and kissed her before leading her to the bedroom.

Gideon closed the door to the bedroom and marched briskly towards Zack. "If you ever pull something like that again, I'll make -," Gideon said before Finnie stepped between them and pointed his finger in Gideon's face.

"Hush. Abby would be a widow right now if not for him. In all the years that I've known you, that was the most sap-headed thing I've ever seen you do. Running straight towards them was sure death. They couldn't have missed if they tried. Not another word unless you want to thank Zack," Finnie said.

Zack watched in astonishment. He had never seen anybody stand up to Gideon like that. People just didn't do it. Nor had he ever seen Finnie take control of a situation with such a commanding presence. The two men continued to eye each other as if neither would back down.

"Let's get the bodies out of here before Winnie gets home. She'll be scared to death," Gideon said and walked out the door.

Finnie winked at Zack before saying, "That was a brave thing that you did. He'll thank you when he comes to his senses."

The two men Finnie shot were dead. The snow had begun to cover their sprawled out bodies and made for peculiar mounds in the yard.

"I shot them in the back. It doesn't look very good upon me," Finnie said as they hoisted the bodies across the backs of the horses.

"They had already tried to kill us and they remained a danger to us and Last Stand. You were just doing your sworn duty," Gideon said.

The horse dragging the body had joined the other horses and the men placed the last body across the saddle.

Finnie grabbed the reins of his horse. "I'll take the bodies on into town. I imagine the people from Paradise will claim them tomorrow and bury them by their church. Zack can help you board up your window. You best stay with Abby."

Gideon smiled at the Irishman. "You'd think that you were the sheriff around here. You're getting bossier than my wife. I hope I don't have to start kissing you too," he said as Finnie led the horses away.

"Only if you close your eyes," Finnie said over his shoulder.

Once the Irishman rode out of sight, Gideon turned to Zack. "He was right, you know. I owe you an apology and a big thank you. I let emotion cloud my better judgement and that's a sure way to get killed."

"It's all forgotten as of this moment. We are family. We better get busy with that window before Chance can play in the snow from inside the cabin," Zack said.

# Chapter 25

Abby and Chance arose from bed after Winnie woke them by bursting into the cabin excited that school would be closed until better weather. She stood covered in snow and shivering. The girl looked up perplexingly towards the boards covering the broken window and then at her frazzled looking mother as she entered the room carrying Chance.

"What's going on?" Winnie asked suspiciously.

Gideon took Chance from Abby's arms and set the boy in front of his sister.

"A bird flew through the window and your momma doesn't feel well. Be a good girl and go play with Chance. I'm going to cook supper tonight," he said.

"Can you really cook?" Winnie asked as Gideon moved to the stove.

"Of course, I can cook. How do you think I survived all those years on the trail," Gideon said.

Sitting down at the table, Abby watched as Winnie took Chance's hand and moved off to play.

"Do you ever get used to it?" Abby asked.

"What's that?" he asked in confusion.

"The killing," she said.

Looking contemplatively at his wife, Gideon tried to form a thoughtful answer. "No, you don't get used to killing, but you come to realize that sometimes it's necessary to survive and prevent more bad things from happening."

"Do you think what I did was necessary?" she asked doubtfully.

"Abby, you saved your families' lives today. If you would've let Gordon get into the cabin, I think it's safe to say that we would have all died. There's nothing more dangerous than a deranged mind that thinks God is on his side," Gideon said and walked over to his wife, helping her from the chair and hugging her.

"I pray that I'm never put in this position again," Abby said as her face puckered up and the tears came.

"I know. I know. We're not going to tell anyone what really happened either. Of course you can tell Sarah and Mary, but the town doesn't need to know what happened. I think it will be easier for you that way," Gideon said.

The family suffered through a chewy beef dinner, and after the meal, Gideon held Abby as they sat on the sofa and watched the children play. He sensed that she was becoming more at peace with herself, but she still seemed vulnerable. Chance began rubbing his eyes and crawled up next to his mother, falling asleep against her. The strain of the day began to wear down Abby and she soon dozed off too. Gideon put them to bed before Winnie roped him into playing checkers until bedtime. She won two of their three games before they called it a night.

The following morning, Abby began crying while frying eggs. The outburst upset Winnie and Chance badly and Gideon was soon trying to deal with three bawling individuals. Abby snapped out of her grieving at seeing the children crying and turned her attention to them while Gideon gladly finished cooking breakfast.

"Are you going to be okay alone? I have to get to town," Gideon said after finishing the meal.

"I'll be fine. The children will keep my mind off things. I'm sorry about this morning," Abby said.

"You're the one that had to suffer through tough eggs because of it," Gideon teased.

"I love you," Abby said.

"Yeah, I'm a keeper. I love you too," Gideon said and kissed his wife.

More than a foot of powdery snow covered the ground. The wind, having abated before the accumulation began in earnest, caused only small drifts in which to navigate Buck around. Cold proved the real hindrance in riding to town and Gideon reached the jail feeling as if he were frozen to the saddle. He found Finnie waiting inside.

"I'm glad you're here. When I rode through town yesterday, there was a couple from Paradise buying supplies and they saw the bodies. The man approached me and wanted to know what happened. I told him that they tried to kill us and they got killed. He didn't seem too pleased with my answer. We should have wrapped up Gordon. I think the man was offended and I fear there'll be trouble today," Finnie said.

"Maybe not. It's damn cold out there. They might stay home and lose their nerve. We're leaving Abby out of this. I killed Gordon if you're asked," Gideon said.

"I figured as much. I got the two short-barreled shotguns ready if needed," Finnie said.

"That's good. How's Mary?" Gideon asked.

"She was still sleeping this morning, but she was good last night. She had me invite Doc over for dinner with us. I think she was worried about him being alone on his first night with John gone and she knew I could use some company after the day we had," Finnie said.

"That's Mary - always thinking of others," Gideon said as he sat.

"What about Abby?" Finnie inquired.

"She's struggling with things. I hope the kids keep her occupied today. I know she'll be okay, but it'll take some time. You know how strong Abby is," Gideon answered.

Finnie poured two cups of coffee and handed one to Gideon.

"Is there anything that you want me to do?" Finnie asked.

"We're going to stay in here and keep as warm as possible. If there's trouble, it can come to us," Gideon said and took a sip.

Mid-morning, the telegraph messenger delivered a telegram to Gideon. Waiting until the man departed, Gideon read the note.

"Our day just got more interesting. James Cooper escaped from the Denver jail and they tracked him south until they lost his trail in heavy snow," Gideon said to Finnie.

"He's coming for us," Finnie said.

"Could be. He said he would and I'd think he'd be headed back east to Missouri otherwise. Maybe we should open the Lucky Horse Saloon back up and retire from this business. You and Mary would have a monopoly going," Gideon said.

"There's days that it seems like we should. I can't imagine you working in a saloon all day long though," Finnie said.

"My pretty face and sunny disposition would probably steal all Mary's business," Gideon joked.

Gideon and Finnie were pulling on their coats to go have lunch at the saloon with Mary when they heard a voice calling from outside. "Sheriff, we want to have a talk with you."

Glancing over at Finnie, Gideon said, "You stand on my right side. If this gets ugly, I'll take out the ringleader and those to my left. You take out the right side. Four rounds of the shotguns should thin the crowd down considerably. Let's hope it doesn't come to that." He then reached into his drawer and pulled out the cross that they found at the first hanging.

Finnie handed Gideon the gun and the two men stepped out of the jail into the cold. About twenty men on horses with rifles resting across their saddles were in front of them. The men were heavily bundled against the weather and looked as if they would have a hard time maneuvering their weapons if called upon. Another man sat on a buckboard with the bodies already loaded in it.

"What can I do for you?" Gideon asked politely.

"We want to know what happened to Pastor Gordon and the other men," the ringleader said.

In a voice free of rancor, Gideon said, "I had suspected that your pastor and the other men were responsible for the hangings of two couples. My deputies and I watched Gordon yesterday and he and the other men rode to my place. A gunfight ensued at the cabin and all of your Paradise men died in that gun battle."

"We know you had it in for Pastor Gordon over the marriage of Charlotte to Cecil Hobbs. We think you murdered him," the man said.

"I didn't like your pastor, but I'm not in the habit of killing people just because I don't like them. I'd probably run out of bullets if I did," Gideon answered.

"We're here to get justice for Pastor Gordon and the other men. We answer to the calling of a higher authority than man's laws. An eye for an eye," the ringleader said.

"You might be able to kill Finnie and me, but I promise you that we will take a hell of a lot of you with us and then your higher authority can figure out who was right and who was wrong. Are you ready to die because you will be the first one?' Gideon said as he pointed the scattergun in the man's direction.

Gideon could see that he had gotten their attention now. The ringleader and the rest of them started looking at one another. The thought of dying caused pause in all but the bravest of men. He didn't figure the Paradise bunch to be of that ilk.

"We're going to contact the U.S. Marshal and demand an investigation," the ringleader said.

"I don't have a problem with that at all. I do want to bring a couple of things to your attention," Gideon said as he pulled the cross from his pocket and held it up for the men to see. "Did any of you notice that Gordon was wearing a new cross? He's probably wearing it now if it wasn't blown to bits. We found this one at the sight of the first hangings. I believe this cross was ripped from his neck there. And another thing, I would think that somebody would have noticed the pastor and the other men riding out on about August twenty-ninth and October third just before a rain and snowstorm and thought it peculiar that the men were leaving with storms setting in. That's when the hangings took place. They did the same thing yesterday."

The men eyed one another again and Gideon could see that his words had stirred memories. At least some of them were putting the pieces of the puzzle together. The ringleader seemed at a loss on what next to do.

"Why would they kill them?" the man finally asked.

"I think it was because the couples were not married. Pastor Gordon seemed to have an obsession with couples living together outside of marriage. I believe he thought he was on a mission from God. He seemed to ignore some of God's other teachings as he saw fit. None of this was your fault. You didn't know," Gideon said.

The fight looked all out of the men now, replaced with self-doubt. Gideon could see in the men's faces that they realized he was right and he hoped by not blaming them, it would allow them to leave with their dignity still intact with no need to try to save face.

The ringleader rubbed the back of his hand against his lips. "We will talk about this back at the church and see what everybody remembers. I know you're right about the cross," he said before turning his horse and riding away with the others in tow.

"Do you think that this is over?" Finnie asked after the men were out of hearing range.

"Oh, yeah, it's over. They realized that I was right. They just have to get used to the idea now," Gideon answered.

"I don't know about you, but all this stare-down nonsense has given me quite the appetite," Finnie said before shivering.

"Let's go get the good doctor and partake ourselves of the fine culinary delights at the Last Chance," Gideon said.

# Chapter 26

The dawn's first light fell on Last Stand as Finnie walked to the jail. Mary's recovery put him in a fine mood and he whistled "Whiskey in the Jar" as he went. He entered the jail and jumped back at seeing a shadowy figure standing by Gideon's desk.

"It's just me, Charlotte. Don't be such a lily liver," she said.

Charlotte stood before him dressed in men's clothing. Suspenders were the only thing holding her gapping pants up and the sleeves of the shirt were rolled up several times. A man's winter coat lay in the chair along with a hat.

Embarrassed by his actions and Charlotte's comment, Finnie barked out, "Standing there in the shadows you looked like one of those scrawny ghosts that roam Ireland. We have lots of them in the old country."

"Well, you must be plenty scared of them the way you jumped," Charlotte said.

"Why are you here?" Finnie asked.

"I ran away again," she said.

"I thought that you were married," he said.

"Depends on what you call marriage. I told you I wouldn't do my wifely duties with Cecil and I kept my word. Every time he got near me, I'd punch him right in his baby-maker. He got to where he walked around with his hand dangling in front of him for protection. He's too embarrassed to tell anybody," Charlotte said.

"By God, you're a mean one alright," Finnie said.

"Since Pastor Gordon and the rest of them got killed, everybody is running around like a chicken with its head cut off. I heard about all of them coming to town. After they figured out that the sheriff told the truth, they just fell apart. They're ashamed. My pa acts like he don't know how they are going to survive. Shoot, they did all the work. Pastor Gordon is the one that had it easy. Nobody will come for me this time," she said.

"I'm sure poor old Cecil won't. You probably ruined him on women for life. Gideon and I tried to get you back, but that wasn't going to happen," Finnie said as he lit the stove.

"Serves Cecil right. I should have a say in who I want to marry," Charlotte said.

"You won't get an argument from me on that point. I like you outfit. Nice and manly," he said.

"Well, I wasn't about to run away in a dress in this weather. I'd like to see you running around in snow with bare legs," she said with irritation.

"You're a lippy thing. I could just throw you in a cell," Finnie said.

"How's Mary?" she asked, ignoring his threat.

"Mary lost the baby and we about lost Mary. She's doing better now, but she's still mourning the loss," Finnie said.

Charlotte seemed taken aback, sorrow showed in her face, and she sat down in the nearest chair. "I'm truly sorry for you and Mary's loss. She's a fine lady and she was good to me. Can I see her?"

"Sure. She was beside herself when you disappeared and she'll be glad to see you. Are you hungry?" he said.

The girl nodded her head.

"Put on your coat. You can see Mary and eat some breakfast," Finnie said and opened the door for her. He admired the girl's spunk if not her mouth.

They walked to the back door of the saloon and went inside. Mary stood cleaning dishes and did a double take as she realized that Finnie's companion was Charlotte. The girl moved quickly to Mary and the two hugged.

"I'm going to fix her some breakfast while you two get caught up," Finnie said.

Finnie listened as Charlotte retold her story to Mary. She had his wife-to-be in stitches with her description of punching Cecil in the baby-maker. He took note that both of them might be dangerous if properly agitated. Mary told the girl about losing the baby and Finnie watched in surprise as the apparently hard-hearted Charlotte teared up.

With the bacon and eggs finished frying, Finnie set the plate in front of the girl. She dug into the food as if days had passed since her last meal. The conversation stalled and Finnie sat beside Mary as they watched the girl devour the food. She mopped up the remaining egg yolk with her bread before looking up and smiling.

"Much obliged. I guess the cold made me hungry," Charlotte said.

"You can have your room back and start helping me until things get figured out. I need someone right now more than ever. That mean old doctor won't let me lift much of anything," Mary said.

Finnie stood. "I'm going back to the jail. I'll be sure to tell the doctor your high opinion of him after he helped save your life."

"Quit being so sensitive. You know that I was joking. If he were younger, I'd marry him instead of you," Mary said before giving Finnie a kiss.

Gideon sat at his desk drinking coffee when Finnie returned.

"About time you showed up," Gideon said.

"Didn't you notice the fire a going? I came in and Charlotte stood waiting at your desk. I took her to Mary. It's a good thing that girl wasn't the ringleader of that Paradise bunch that showed up here. We'd had a shootout for sure if she was," Finnie said.

Smiling, Gideon said, "I expect that you're right. I got a letter from the sheriff in Toledo last week. He found her uncle and they agreed to take her in. Whether she will go will be the next thing. You're liable to have a permanent resident at the saloon."

"Oh, pity me if that's true. That girl has a mean streak, but she can also be quite sweet when the mood strikes her. Wait until you hear her story," Finnie said as he poured a cup of coffee and took a seat, ready for some gossip.

Finnie yapped all morning to the point that Gideon stood ready to brave the cold to get away from him. As much as he was tired of hearing the Irishman talk, he couldn't help but be happy that his friend sounded like himself again. The more Mary recovered, the more Finnie talked and laughed.

"I'm going to the saloon to get lunch. You stay here and watch things," Gideon said.

"Aren't we going together?" Finnie asked.

"No, my ears need a break. You can get Doc to go with you and wear him out," Gideon said.

"That's a fine thing to say to somebody that risks his life with you. If you were a dog you'd probably bite the man that fed you a bone and then hike your leg up on him," Finnie said.

Ignoring him, Gideon said, "Have you and Mary set a date yet?"

"As soon as she's all well, we're going to get Ethan to do the honor. You better get your Sunday coat ready," Finnie said.

"There's no accounting for the taste some women have in men," Gideon said as he opened the door to leave.

"Well, she had eyes for you before I ever lived here," Finnie shouted as Gideon slammed the door shut.

Grinning all the way to the saloon, Gideon sat down at his usual table. His arrival was early and the place had yet to fill with patrons. Charlotte, now wearing a dress, brought him a beer and a plate of food.

"I see I have you to deal with again," he said.

"You like me and you know it," Charlotte said.

"Sit down a minute. I need to talk to you," he said.

Charlotte looked around and sat after determining that she wasn't needed anywhere for the moment. "What is it?" she asked.

"I got a letter from Toledo. They found an uncle of yours and you can go live with them if you like," Gideon said.

The girl looked surprised by the news and didn't say anything for a moment. "Really? Do I have to go live with them?"

"No, you're free to do what you want. If you stay, you'll have to figure out things. I don't know that Mary will be able to keep you on forever. You'd have to talk to her about that," Gideon said before taking a bite of boiled pork.

"And the marriage?" Charlotte inquired.

"I'm going to take a walk to the recording office. I have a hunch that the record of Cecil and you obtaining a marriage license might have disappeared and if it's ever returned to be recorded as a marriage, that might disappear too," Gideon said.

"You'd do that for me?" she asked.

Gideon smiled. "I didn't say that I was doing anything. I just told you my hunch."

"Thank you. There's a lot to think about," Charlotte said.

"Why didn't you tell the truth and come with us when we rode out to Paradise to get you?" Gideon asked.

"Because Pastor Gordon told me that he would make my fourteen-year-old sister marry Cecil if I didn't and I thought that I'd get you and Finnie killed if I tried to go with you. I wasn't about to let either thing happen," Charlotte said.

Mary came out of the back room, and on seeing Gideon, walked to the table. "Are you trying to keep my help from doing her job?" she asked.

"Well, aren't you looking pretty? You look just about healthy enough to start chasing that blabbering Irishman with a frying pan," Gideon said.

Mary sat down at the table. "He has been talkative, but I have to be nice. I can tell that I scared the devil out of him and he's treating me like a queen. Sometimes he acts as if I'm going to break in two."

Gideon took a swig of beer. "So how are you doing?"

"I'm getting better, but some days are harder than others. I still have a hard time accepting that I lost the baby. After years of thinking I couldn't have one and then to lose it, it's just too much. I wonder if I'll ever get another chance," Mary said and forced a smile.

"I'm betting on you. The world needs another little Finnie running around," Gideon said, making Mary laugh.

"Speaking of the little Irish devil, there he and Doc are," Mary said as the two men entered the saloon.

"Good God, I told him to wait. Now I'll have to listen to him some more while I eat," he said before taking a big gulp of beer.

# Chapter 27

The weather turned unseasonably warm for the last week of October. All of the snow melted away and the streets of Last Stand turned into a mud bog. Boards laid across the street made crossing from one side to the other possible. Wagons left deep ruts and horses plodded to their destination.

Mary and Finnie were digging into plates of eggs, sausage, and biscuits with gravy. Afterwards, she planned to go see Sarah for her first Wednesday visit since her illness. Doc would not hear of her riding a horse, but had reluctantly agreed that she could take a buggy. She had no idea whether Sarah would be expecting company or if Abby would be there, but she desperately needed out of the saloon. Between convalescing, liver, the weather, and Finnie's smothering attention, she needed some time for herself.

"Are you sure you're ready to go out?" Finnie asked.

"Finnie, I feel fine. I'm almost back to good as new," Mary replied.

"Well, are you ready to set a date to get married then?" he said.

The question made her smile. She had secretly feared that now that she had lost the baby and felt better, Finnie would get cold feet about a wedding. "If Ethan can do it, let's get married on Saturday."

Finnie held up his coffee cup and toasted with Mary. "To the future Mrs. Ford," he said.

Taking a bite of sausage, Mary chewed it methodically before speaking. "I've been thinking that maybe we should buy the Lucky Horse. This place is making so much more money since that place closed and one of these days somebody will buy it and cut our business. If we own it, somebody would have to build a new saloon from scratch."

"Won't we be competing against ourselves if we run two saloons," Finnie said.

"I wouldn't make it a saloon. We could rent it out as a store, or what I'd really like to do is make it a restaurant. The hotel is the only place men can take their wives to eat and I know that we could beat their prices. Delta could run it and we could get out of the whoring business. I've no stomach for it anymore," she said.

"Listen to my little business baron. You've really thought this out," he said before taking a sip of coffee.

"I have. I'm also beginning to think Charlotte won't go to Ohio. She could work at both places. I think we could pull it off," Mary said and smiled.

"What about when we have a baby?" Finnie asked.

Mary smiled at him again and her eyes moistened. "Finnegan Ford, I do love you. We'll figure it out as we go."

"We have my reward money that we can use to buy it," Finnie offered.

"I've been saving money too. We should be able to buy it cheap. Nobody else has put a bid in on it," Mary said.

"I could still be Gideon's deputy, couldn't I?" Finnie asked.

"Of course. Somebody has to keep him alive," she joked.

"I think it best that I let you run things. I know my strengths," he said.

"Finnie, I've been wondering something and I've been half afraid to ask. When I was talking out of my head, did I say anything embarrassing?" Mary asked.

Finnie smiled mischievously at her. "Mary, I can't recall a thing that you said that was improper. It was all just nonsense."

Looking at him warily, she wasn't sure whether he was teasing. She decided that maybe it best she did not know and decided not to pursue the subject any further. "I've got to go. I'm ready to see Sarah," she said.

∞

Abby stood dressed and ready to go see Sarah. She had no idea whether Joann would even realize that it was Wednesday, let alone think to come watch Chance because of the change in the weather. Peeking out the window, she saw her daughter riding up on her horse. A smile came to her face not only for the fact that she was getting out of the cabin, but also for the pride that swelled up in her at seeing her daughter. Joann looked lovely and had matured into a fine woman.

"Thank goodness you remembered. I've been pacing the floor wondering," Abby said.

"I thought of you first thing this morning. How are you doing?" Joann asked.

"I guess I'm doing the same as I was when I saw you at church on Sunday. I'm fine sometimes and sometimes not. At least Gideon got the window replaced. That helps," Abby said.

Chance walked over to his sister and she picked him up.

"Did you know that when the pastor ran behind the cabin to try to get through the window that Zack had to tackle Daddy to keep him from running straight into the gunfire? Zack said he would have been shot for sure," Joann said.

"No, no one told me that. I'm not surprised," Abby answered, shaking her head.

"Afterward, Daddy was going to let Zack have it and Finnie stepped between them and put a stop to it. Zack couldn't believe it. He'd never seen anybody stand up to Daddy like that, let alone it be Finnie," Joann said.

"Good for both of them. Gideon forgets sometimes that he's a mere mortal. He needs somebody to look out for him and keep him in line besides me," Abby said with a chuckle.

"Abs, on the subject of men, does it ever get any easier living with them? Zack and I are happy and all, but there are times when I'd like to strangle him. He slurps his coffee when it's too hot and he drops his clothes wherever he takes them off. It's just little things, but it about drives me crazy sometimes," Joann said.

Abby smiled and let out a sigh. "You'll get used to their little annoying habits in time. Remember that we have them too. I drive Gideon nuts by leaving drawers open an inch. I do it without even thinking. I don't know why I don't push them in all the way. Age does wonders for your tolerance too. Zack Barlow has far more good points than bad," Abby said in defense of her son-in-law.

"I guess you're right. I'll have to remember this conversation the next time I want to kill him. Get going and go have some fun. Chance and I will play up a storm," Joann said.

Abby picked up the apple pie that she had baked and placed it in a basket. She always took Joann's horse on her trip and she looped the basket onto the saddle horn with a string she'd tied to it.

Having a horse beneath her again felt good. Abby had always loved to ride and she felt free of her burdens for the moment. She avoided the roads as much as possible and traveled across pastures where the footing remained firm. Arriving at Sarah's cabin just as Mary pulled up in a buggy, the two women grinned at each other.

"I hope Sarah is expecting us," Abby called out.

Sarah walked out onto the porch. "It's about time that you two got here. I was going to lose my mind if I didn't have a conversation with somebody besides Ethan."

The women went inside the cabin and the two guests sat down at the table while Sarah brewed a fresh pot of coffee. They busied themselves with small talk until Sarah filled their cups.

Abby blurted, "Did you know I killed Pastor Gordon? He tried to get into the cabin."

Sarah and Mary paused in mid-sip and exchanged glances.

Sarah set her cup down on the table. "I'm sorry. I didn't know that. But you had to protect yourself. That probably doesn't make taking a life any easier, but you have to know you did the right thing."

"I keep telling myself that and it helps sometimes, but I took the life of another human being and a preacher to top it off. Gideon thought it best not to let many people know the truth," Abby said.

Mary reached over and patted Abby's arm. "Finnie never told me. When I killed that gambler, Hiatt, in the saloon, I kept telling myself that if I hadn't done it that Gideon would've been killed and then I would've been next. That's what got me through it. Sometimes there's no other choice and I finally just quit thinking about it. I wish things could have been different, but I feel no guilt whatsoever now. His death was preferable to ours."

Hiatt had been a gambler that came to town in pursuit of the Last Chance. He murdered the previous owner and after Mary inherited the saloon, he had tried to force her to sell. After beating and badly cutting Mary, Gideon became aware of the plot and a gunfight ensued. Mary killed the gambler after he had Gideon pinned down behind a table in the saloon.

"I should've never looked at the body. I can't get that out of my head," Abby said.

"I tried to make myself think of something good every time I did that. Make yourself think of Chance when it happens," Mary said.

Abby took a sip of coffee. "Thank both of you for listening. It helps to talk about it and I'm sure I'll get through this like everything else in life. I'll try what Mary says, but enough about me. Anybody else have some news?" she asked.

Grinning like a Cheshire cat, Mary said, "I hear that if a certain preacher is available this Saturday, there's going to be a wedding," she said.

Abby and Sarah let out whoops and hollers before congratulating Mary.

"Don't worry about the preacher. I'll make darn sure he's available," Sarah said.

The three women spent the rest of their time together planning, reminiscing, and giggling about weddings. All the talking seemed to spur their appetites and they dove into the pie and Mary's cookies as if famished.

Abby finished a cookie, and said, "If we ate like this every day, our men would be kicking us out of the bed."

"Speak for yourself. I could get as fat as a pig and still make Ethan beg," Sarah said to an eruption of laughter.

Ethan walked into the cabin while the women were still laughing. "What's so funny?" he asked.

The women all looked at one another and broke out into another fit of giggling.

"Honey, there's some things that it's best you just don't know about," Sarah said.

# Chapter 28

Saturday morning found Sarah already aflutter trying to decide which dress she would wear to the wedding that afternoon. She had talked about her choices all through breakfast and continued as she cleared the table. Years ago, Ethan had perfected the art of giving supportive generic answers when asked his opinion on clothing choices. He never replied with much more than "You look good in that" or "That dress shows off your figure." Sarah didn't seem to notice that he never actually helped her with a decision and she would eventually pick out her choice.

Benjamin left to do his chores without prompting. No good usually came his way when his mother got worked up. Somehow, it usually turned into extra work for him.

Ethan stood up from the table. "I have to run to the barn. I'll be right back."

Sarah waved her hand at him to go and turned her attention to washing the dishes.

The day before, Ethan had gone to town for feed and to check on the china and ring he had ordered for Sarah. Both gifts had arrived from Denver. He hid the crate of dishes behind the sacks of feed and debated giving the gifts to her that night before opting for Saturday.

Carrying the crate to the cabin took all the brawn that he could muster and he shouted for Sarah to open the door.

"What in the world is that?" she asked as he sat the box on the floor.

Retrieving a hammer, Ethan popped the wooden lid loose. "Have a look for yourself," he said.

Carefully removing the packaging, Sarah spied a blue willow plate. "What have you done?" she asked.

"I bought you a complete set of china. Eight settings. I figured we could use some of the reward money to spruce things up a little," Ethan said.

Sarah held the plate in her hand, looking at it and then to her husband. For once in her life, she was near speechless. "For me? Ethan Oakes, I don't know what I'm going to do with you. You outdid yourself this time," she said and carefully set the plate down before hugging her husband.

"I got one more surprise. You can wear it with whatever dress you decide on," he said and pulled the small box from his coat pocket.

Taking the box from Ethan, Sarah slowly opened it. A small gasp escaped her and she put the pearl ring onto her finger. Tearing up, she couldn't talk. She waved her hand through the air while Ethan smiled at her as if it were the best day of his life.

"Do you like it?" Ethan finally asked.

"Of course, I love it. Sometimes you're just too good to me. This is the most thoughtful thing that you have ever done. And it's such a surprise. I can't wait to show the girls," she said and hugged him again.

Benjamin walked into the cabin and saw his parents hugging.

"Look what your pa got me," Sarah said and proudly held out her hand to show off her ring. "And look at our new dishes."

The boy stared at the ring and dishes before glancing at the smiles on his parents' faces. His pa looked as happy as his momma did, and he wondered about that. The Bible verse that said it was better to give than receive came to mind and he thought he understood it for the first time. He decided that from now on he would have to do better with picking out presents. "I don't have a present for you, but I'll help you pick out a dress."

"You got a deal," Sarah said. "Now help me unpack the china so that we can see the rest of it."

∞

Gideon's family ran around the cabin trying to get ready for the wedding. They needed to leave soon and Chance was still walking around in his diaper. Abby chased after him with outfit in hand while Gideon retrieved a brush for Winnie's hair. The child preferred her stepfather to do the job over her mother's rougher approach. He never pulled her hair.

Once the hair was brushed, Gideon pulled a box out of his pocket. "Go give this to your mother when she's finished with Chance. Tell her we got her a surprise."

The necklace had finally come in on the same shipment as Ethan's ring and china. Hiram had brought it to the jail with the picture already in the locket. The engraving had held up the delivery, but the workmanship had been worth the wait.

Abby finished tying Chance's boot while Winnie waited anxiously by her side.

"What is it, Winnie? We have to go," Abby said.

Winnie moved her hand from behind her back and held out the box. "We got you a surprise," she said.

Abby took the box and looked up at Gideon as he walked over to them.

"What have you done?" Abby asked.

"Open it and find out," he said.

Opening the box, Abby careful lifted the locket. "It has my initials on it and it's gold," she said with astonishment.

Gideon leaned down and showed her how to open the cover. She saw the picture and put her hand over her mouth in shock.

"When did you get this picture taken?" she asked.

Winnie said, "Joann took us to town. We surprised you, didn't we?"

"I would say so," Abby replied.

"Being sheriff, I know how to arrange covert activities," Gideon said.

Abby put on the locket. "This is just about the best present ever," she said and hugged Winnie and then Gideon before wiping the moisture from her eyes with the back of her hand. "You know how to make a girl feel special, but we got to go."

∞

Much to the chagrin of townsfolk and cowboys, a note was stuck on the Last Chance stating that the saloon would not open until six o'clock on Saturday. Mary stood upstairs in the bedroom looking at herself in the mirror. She wore a new store bought dress that she had purchased that week. The dress was off-white in color with lace around the neckline and showed off her figure. Delta came into the room to help her fix her hair. They had one hour before they needed to leave for Ethan's church.

Finnie paced downstairs behind the bar. His new coat and trousers felt stiff and his string tie seemed as if it were trying to choke him. The whiskey bottle tempted him for one of the few times since he had given it up, but rather than break his word, he settled for a glass of beer. He still couldn't believe that he, Finnegan Ford, stood on the threshold of marriage and he wished Gideon were sitting with him to have a talk.

Mary insisted that Finnie couldn't see her in her dress before the wedding so he rode with Doc to the church and Mary came with Delta and Charlotte. Ethan, Sarah, and Benjamin were waiting at the church and Gideon and his family soon arrived. Zack and Joann were the last to arrive at the church.

Pulling Gideon to the side as they waited to begin the ceremony, Finnie said, "Gideon, do you think I'm doing the right thing? Mary could do so much better than me. I feel she's sold herself short," he said.

"Oh, good God, will you stop. I assure you that Mary Sawyer would not be marrying you unless that is what she wants. You bring out the best in each other. Finnie, you're a good man. Just be happy that you've found somebody after all this time. And besides, I'll shoot you dead if you get cold feet now," Gideon said.

"I guess I just needed to hear that. It's still hard thinking of me as a married man. Let's do this," Finnie said.

Sarah insisted that her mother's blue sapphire ring brought good luck and placed it on Mary's finger.

"You make a beautiful bride and I'm so happy for you and Finnie. You'll have a wonderful life together and don't lose faith, I know there'll be a baby one of these days," Sarah said.

Mary smiled. "Who would have ever thought my life would turn out this way? I need to pinch myself to make sure it's real."

The guest took their seats. Gideon stood at the front of the church with Finnie. Delta walked down the aisle as the maid of honor, and as everybody arose, Mary followed arm-in-arm with Doc. Finnie's goofy grin would have annoyed the bride if it wasn't so sincere and she winked at him.

Ethan cleared his throat. "Hello, everybody. The nice thing about this small wedding today is that we are all friends here. We can be more informal and personal. We've seen each other at their best and their worst and yet we choose to call each other friend. Finnie and Mary have been dealt blows in life that would have felled lesser people, but they persevered through it all and stand here today ready to become husband and wife in the eyes of the Lord and start a new life together. Every time I look at Mary, I can't help but think of the blessings she brought to my family. I could never repay the debt that I owe her. And for Finnie, his life has been richly rewarded for the changes he has made since moving to Last Stand. I'm honored to call him one of my dearest friends. They are both shining examples to all of us to never give up, but to greet each day and try to make it better. Mary and Finnie are two of the people that make Last Stand a special place and I believe with all my heart that God's hand is in everything that brought us all together here today. Let us pray."

After the prayer, Ethan stuck to his usual wedding ceremony. After telling Finnie that he could kiss the bride, he said, "Ladies and gentlemen, I'd like to introduce Mr. and Mrs. Finnegan Ford."

Everybody stood and clapped and the crusty old doctor got misty eyed when Mary gave him a little wave on the way out of the church. After all the congratulations were made, the group headed to the Last Chance.

Ethan had not been in the saloon since he became a preacher except for the funeral of the old owner, Mr. Vander. There was a time when he wouldn't have gone in, but with all the good and bad that had happened in the last couple of years, he just didn't care what people thought any longer. His conscience would be his guide. He took Sarah by the arm and walked through the entrance with Benjamin following behind them.

Delta and Charlotte scrambled to the back, bringing out food and setting it on the bar. Once they finished, Delta took over as the bartender.

"Okay, everybody, we have three hours before the saloon opens. Eat and drink up," Mary announced.

Benjamin and Winnie stood in the corner whispering. They were in awe of the saloon. The long carved bar looked fancier than anything that they had ever seen in their lives and the mirrors and bottles of liquor behind it looked mesmerizing. Much to their delight, Mary walked over to them and handed each a bag of candy.

Three tables were butted together and everybody sat around them eating boiled pork and stewed potatoes while washing it down with beer. Benjamin and Winnie were exploring behind the bar and too busy stuffing candy into their mouths to care about the others while their mothers covertly sipped brews. Joann eyed her parents warily, she didn't know what they'd think of her drinking beer, but she had never tried it and she wasn't about to pass up the opportunity.

Gideon stood and raised his glass. "A toast," he said. "May Finnie and Mary have a long, happy life together. They deserve it."

All the mugs clinked together as Chance watched with fascination from his mother's lap at all the festivities.

Finnie turned to Doc. "You're the only one that hasn't gotten married. Maybe you'll be next."

Doc waved his hand at the Irishman. "I'm too old for a young one and too spry for an old one," he said to an explosion of laughter.

The reception proved to be a lively affair with lots of laughter and storytelling. Sarah and Abby both made it a point to show off their new jewelry and brag on their husbands. Just before six o'clock, the party broke up. Sarah, Abby, and Joann all stood up to find that they were a little wobbly. They started giggling as if their condition was the funniest thing on earth. Gideon took Chance from his mother and offered her an arm to steady herself.

"We can't take you girls anywhere," Gideon teased.

Joann whispered something in Zack's ear and his face turned red.

Sarah watched the exchange. Never known for her shyness even when sober, she said, "I bet I know what's going on. Zack don't run that horse in the ground trying to hurry home. Sometimes us women like a long, slow ride. You can thank me for the talk that I had with Joann before your wedding."

Zack's face turned so red that his ears burned and Joann hid behind her hands.

Ethan grabbed his wife's elbow. "Let's get you home before you say something that you will regret," he said and winked at Zack, further embarrassing the young man.

Delta and Charlotte began clearing the bar of food and glasses after the guests departed while Mary crawled into Finnie's lap.

"Are you ready to go seal the deal?" Mary asked.

# Chapter 29

With the coffee freshly brewed, Finnie poured cups for himself, Doc, and Gideon. The three men sat in the jail shooting the breeze after lunch at the Last Chance. Finnie could still barely contain himself over his and Mary's nuptials. Doc and Gideon sneaked smiles and rolled their eyes between themselves as the Irishman railed on about his happiness. The dissertation on the joys of marriage was interrupted by the arrival of the telegraph messenger.

After the messenger had gone, Gideon said, "That was from Marshall Wilcox. James Cooper was spotted in Alamosa. He robbed a general store and stole a horse there yesterday."

"That's only about a day's ride away. He's coming," Finnie said.

"Yes, he is," Gideon said as he tossed the note onto his desk.

"Are you worried?" Finnie asked.

"What's the point? It wouldn't do any good. What's going to happen will happen," Gideon said.

"I'm worried about another ambush like when Ike Todd tried to kill you from the hotel window," Finnie said.

"I don't think Cooper will do that. He has his reputation as a supposedly fast gun to protect. He wouldn't want to read in the papers how he cowardly ambushed a sheriff," Gideon said and took a sip of coffee.

"You don't think he's that fast?" Finnie asked.

"I have no idea. You don't have to be fast to gun down bank tellers and train engineers in cold blood," Gideon said.

Doc rubbed his chin and pulled off his spectacles. "This world would be a lot better place if people just went about their lives doing the right thing."

"That it would, but too many people are just no damn good," Finnie said.

"With the philosophical teachings of Finnegan Ford now firmly in my head, I'm going to go see patients. Who needs Aristotle?" Doc said and stood.

"I'm not sure what you just said, but I believe that I've been insulted," Finnie said.

The doctor paused at the door. "How can you be insulted if you don't know what I'm talking about?" he said and walked out before there could be a reply.

"You would think that old goat's heart would have been softened by meeting his son," Finnie said. "I have to go get Mary. With the judge in town, we're going to go see if he'll accept our bid on the Lucky Horse."

The Lucky Horse Saloon had been seized by the state when Gideon had arrested the owners for running a sex slave operation. The building had sat empty since that time after no bids were received to purchase it.

"Really? Are you and Mary planning to buy up the town?" Gideon asked.

"She thinks we could make a successful restaurant out of it," Finnie answered.

"Mary is a smart one. She'll be making so much money that you'll quit on me and sit around getting fat," Gideon said.

"I doubt that. I've been told by more than one person that it's my job to keep you alive," Finnie said before leaving.

Finnie and Mary had to wait their turn to present a bid to Judge Laurel for the Lucky Horse. In Mary's absence, Delta bartended while Charlotte dusted the bottles behind the bar. A few patrons milled about and flirted with Delta to pass the time.

James Cooper walked into the bar and scanned the crowd. Some of the men gave him a glance, but none showed any signs of recognition. He swaggered up to the bar and ordered a glass of whiskey.

"Are you new in town?" Delta asked.

The outlaw smiled. "I've been here once before," he said and turned his attention to sipping his drink.

Cooper nursed the whiskey before tipping the glass back and killing off the last of the drink. "Hey, little lady," he called out to Charlotte as she squatted on the floor while restocking bottles. "I've got a five dollar gold piece here for you if you go tell the sheriff that James Cooper will be waiting for him out in the street." He popped a gold coin down on the bar.

Standing, Charlotte looked at the coin and then to Delta. The bartender tilted her head towards the door and the girl scampered out. James Cooper ordered another whiskey. He killed the drink in one long gulp and walked out of the saloon.

Charlotte burst into the jail out of breath and found Gideon sitting at his desk cleaning a rifle.

"Sheriff, there's a man in the saloon named James Cooper and he told me to come tell you that he'd meet you in the street," Charlotte blurted out before gasping for air.

Gideon sat back in his chair, rubbed his scar, and took a big breath that he blew out with inflated cheeks. "Thank you, Charlotte."

"Is he here to kill you?" the girl asked.

"He is. He's an outlaw and I killed his brother," Gideon answered.

"What are you going to do?" Charlotte asked.

Gideon smiled. "Let's hope that I kill him instead of the other way around. You stay in here until this is over," he said as he arose from his desk. Out of habit, he worked his revolver up and down in the holster until satisfied that it moved smoothly.

Finnie and Mary had left the courtroom feeling on top of the world. Judge Laurel hadn't been pleased with a bid of five hundred dollars, but he nonetheless accepted the offer with the stipulation that back taxes be paid. The couple sauntered to the jail to retrieve the keys to the locked up saloon. Finnie looked down the street and spotted James Cooper standing in the middle of it just as he and Mary reached the jail door. Gideon opened it at that moment and Finnie hooked an arm around Mary's waist and bulled into the jail, pushing Gideon with him as they went through the door.

"Cooper is out there," Finnie said.

"I know. He sent word for me. I'm going out there to face him," Gideon said.

"Damn it, Gideon, we're the law. The outlaws don't get to tell us how to capture them - we do. One of us can draw a bead on him at the window and the other at the door. There'll probably be no bloodshed that way. We can take him alive. There's no need to risk your life," Finnie said.

"Finnie, I can't run from a challenge. I've got to face him. What would the town think?" Gideon said.

"Since when did you give a damn about what anybody thought about you? And I'd hope that they'd think that they have a pretty smart sheriff. It sure beats them thinking about how silly you were for walking out into the street and getting yourself killed and leaving behind a widow and children," Finnie said.

"Finnie, just let it go," Gideon said and started to walk past the deputy.

Mary stepped in front of Gideon, blocking his path to the door. "Gideon Johann, you're not running from a challenge. You are facing it on your own terms. Finnie is right. Why let Cooper make the rules? You are the sheriff, not a gunfighter. I swear to God if you go out there I'll never speak to you again whether you're dead or alive."

Gideon grinned at her. "I wish I had a few more bossy women in my life. I'd never have to make a decision ever again if I did."

Not trusting him, Mary remained firmly planted at the door.

"What'll it be?" Finnie asked.

Gideon let out a big sigh. "Get two rifles. We'll do it your way. Mary might scratch my eyes out and I'd have to face Cooper blind otherwise."

Finnie retrieved two Winchesters from the rack and checked their loads before handing one to Gideon.

"You two women go back in the cell room," Finnie said.

Still standing by the door, Mary asked, "Do I have your word that you are doing it Finnie's way?"

"Yes, I'm not about to trick you. I'd never hear the end of it. Now get your butt back there," Gideon commanded.

Finnie opened the window. "Are you ready?"

Gideon nodded before flinging the door open and taking aim from the cover of the wall.

"Cooper, there's two Winchesters aimed at you. Throw down your gun," Gideon yelled.

"Well, you yellow belly coward. I thought that you were a man. I planned on giving you a fair chance and you won't do me the same," Cooper yelled.

"This is your last chance. Now throw down your gun," Gideon hollered.

Cooper paused and seemed not to know what next to do. He scanned both sides of the street before drawing his gun and firing at the jail while running towards a water trough. The two Winchesters roared simultaneously and Cooper did a little skip like a young girl playing hopscotch before dropping to the ground face first and not moving.

Gideon watched from the doorway until satisfied that Cooper was dead. Without looking back, he listened to Mary and Charlotte come barreling out of cell room. Time seemed to have slowed and his senses felt hyperactive. The clock ticking on the wall sounded like a drum and he could feel his pulse beating in his temples. He inhaled slowly and released the tension as he exhaled.

Finnie called out, "Don't get in my line of fire. I'm going to keep a bead on him until you get out there."

Walking slowly toward the body, Gideon kept his hand resting on his revolver until he stepped close enough to see two exit wounds in the back close to where the heart and lungs would be located. He kicked the gun away and squatted down to check for a pulse. James Cooper lay dead.

Gideon stood up, looking down the street and then back down at the body. The sight made him wonder about his own life choices and how different things might have turned out if he and his pa had never volunteered for the war. He probably would have ended up a rancher like Ethan and may have never taken a man's life. None of that really mattered anyhow because that path had not been taken and he couldn't change any of it now. Conjecture was just a waste of his time. The two things that he knew for sure were that he was tired of killing and that he had his fill of being sheriff for that day. He just wanted to go home to be with Abby and his family.

# About the Author

Duane Boehm is a musician, songwriter, and author. He lives on a mini-farm with his wife and an assortment of dogs. Having written short stories throughout his lifetime, he shared them with friends and with their encouragement, he has written his fifth novel *Last Ride*. Please feel free to email him at boehmduane@gmail.com or like his Facebook Page www.facebook.com/DuaneBoehmAuthor.

Made in the USA
Lexington, KY
10 September 2016